Prologue:

This would be the last time. He had promised himself that many

times before - but this would be the last time. Slowly, he drew back

his sleeve to reveal a forearm ravaged by a thousand previous

promises. The tube was tight above his elbow and the fluid, even

now, began to create a new reality, beyond the mundane, without

rhyme or reason. Most importantly, without reason. For once he

was right, this was the last time.

It was just another Thursday. Far enough into the week to make

the weekend a tantalising prospect, but not close enough to begin

the ritual of self-abuse that had become his only form of

relaxation. It was just another body. Younger than most, but still just another body. The forensic guys had finished long ago, but it didn't take a genius to work out the cause of death. It was virtually routine. Mind-numbing, soulless routine.

There had been a time when a death as young as this one would have caused concern in the department, hell there had been a time when even Sean would have been concerned. Before the day job had taken its toll, before the mind numbing soulless routine had become his life. He watched now as the zip closed over a young face that would not see another dawn and probably didn't care.

Now, it was his turn. His turn to try to piece together the fragments of a life and find somebody to blame. It didn't matter who, just so long as the file had a name at the end it really didn't matter whose it was. Nobody gave a damn how it started anymore, just get somebody to blame. His experience showed that the kids didn't Just say 'no', most of them just said 'yes' and never looked back.

Even for Sean, there were times when that attitude had its attractions. It sure as hell would cut down on the paperwork.

Aside from the obvious, he hadn't a lot to go on. Sean smiled involuntarily. It was hardly funny but laughs were hard to come by just at present. Sean examined the scene. He had seen hundreds just like it. The discarded needle lay close by where the body had lain propped against the dumpster amid the rotting remains of yesterday's garbage and tomorrow's news. It didn't look as though the streets had been swept in living memory (which was a mixed blessing) - nothing to disturb the evidence, but everything covered in a grime which no amount of washing could remove. Anyway, like the man said, it didn't take a genius to work out what had happened.

"Have we got a name", asked Sean to nobody in particular.

"Nothing as yet",

came the reply from an older man who appeared out of the crowd which had rapidly appeared soon after the sound of wailing sirens had filled the street. As usual, nobody had seen anything (nobody ever saw anything). Sean dismissed the thought and turned back to his partner, who continued to scan his notebook for some time, searching for some information which was obviously not there.

Sean had never liked Harry since he had been first assigned to him. Harry was one of the old school. Part of the DEA since the early days, a process man, keen on procedure and clearly going no further. Just waiting out his pension, trying not to get killed.

"Kid over here reckons he works up at the plant."

Big deal , who didn't work up at the plant, that was like saying that tomorrow would be Friday. Harry, expert in the bleedin' obvious.

"Well, that narrows it down to just over nine thousand then."

Sean had given up trying up to hide his distaste for his partner, who was anything but when it came to the things that really mattered. Slowly he took out a cigarette and put it to his lips, he knew it would probably kill him, but like everything else, Sean didn't really care. The smoke felt good in his lungs as he dragged out an answer,

"I guess we'll start up there, then."

Sean knew it would be fruitless, the plant provided the only employment there was in the area and the suits up there weren't about to admit to a drug problem no matter what the evidence.

Steve had to admit() life wasn't bad. Not terrific, but definitely not bad. He relaxed in his chair and kicked off his shoes. Yes, things were going okay. He would make his target next month, as he had for the last four months, and pretty soon he would be moving on up. The trip had proved his worth and at last he was being noticed. He had noticed that things had started to become a little easier now, nobody parked behind him in the car park any more and his opinion had been sought out in many areas which before had definitely been off limits. Clearly, his name was getting about and that could only be good.

Steve Gaynor was twenty-seven, recently promoted, young for his position but well respected by the political in-crowd. Most of that was down to riding the political coat tails of the company's youngest ever director and a particularly successful sales trip to Europe a few months before when he had tied up a distribution deal which had provided much needed volume at a time when things were not exactly looking rosy. Steve liked to think that it was more to do with the latter, besides which, he would be a director himself soon enough. If truth be told, there had been a few times on that trip when even Steve had begun to doubt that he could pull it off, but somehow it had all dropped into place with very little help from his direction. He had, naturally, kept this last detail to himself (why not take the credit, he had reasoned). True, he wasn't exactly sure of the background to his new distributor, but he was taking eight-hundred vehicles a year and that was all that matted. Eight-hundred units at thirty thousand pounds a time would do very nicely thank you.

Aside from his minor role in the transaction there were two further details which Steve had decided to keep to himself. his own two per cent commission on every vehicle which was building up nicely in Zurich and then of course there was Terry. He was definitely going to keep Terry to himself.

Anyway, why should he worry, eight hundred units, rising to twelve hundred if things panned out. And things were going to pan out if Steve had anything to do with it. Despite Steve's ignorance of the detail of the deal, he did know that it had proved somewhat of a coup. To the outside world, he had opened up the European market and the potential was vast. By a simple counter trade deal, Steve had secured a substantial starting volume at realistic prices and established a distribution bridgehead which could only get better. In his dreams, Steve foresaw the day when the North-East of England would become the centre of European Operations; the gateway to France, Spain, Germany, Italy and beyond. Eight hundred units at thirty thousand a piece. Eight hundred units earning him two percent a time. Yeah, life was okay.

Now that he came to think about it, Steve wasn't exactly sure when Terry had come onto the scene. They had got together at the party which had followed the signing of the deal , that much he did know. To be honest, you didn't forget a night like that in a hurry but Steve was vaguely aware that she had been around before and was close to convincing himself that they had met on the plane going over, but as with so much, that detail had escaped him. Either way, you didn't forget a night like that in a hurry and there had been many such nights since, so how they had met was not important, fact was they were together and that was good enough.

Following the signing ceremony and the party to end all parties, Steve had felt secure enough to take a few days holiday (he was owed enough, after all), and it had seemed perfectly natural for Terry to show him the sights. Four days later, she had come back with him back to the States and taken up residence in his apartment as if it was the most natural thing in the world. She would be waiting for him now.

Steve eased his shoes back on, put on his jacket, slipped past his secretary and headed for home. He eased into his Cherokee, coaxed the engine into life and settled into the seat as Oleta Adams started to warble provocatively from over his left shoulder. The freeway was quiet now, the first flood of commuters long since dissipated into the seaboard heartlands. The Cherokee cruised effortlessly towards Annapolis, skirting the docks and the less salubrious areas of Washington. If you tried hard enough, you could ignore the central city depravation and see only the better elements of a life in the nation's capital. Steve was an old hand - he could see just what he wanted to see - it was easy.

A little after eight, the streamlined nose of the Cherokee eased into a tree-lined driveway in the suburbs. Sure enough, Terry was there to meet him. As he opened the door, she was melting into his arms, her lean body pressing ever closer, her tongue seeking out his lips and darting between them provocatively. Steve struggled to close the door under the onslaught but was only too keen to give himself

over to pleasure and put up little resistance as Terry became more

insistent and began to lead him towards the den. The den had been

her idea and as they surrendered themselves to the soft cushions

Steve had cause to thank his lucky stars once more.

Afterwards, in the silence she reached for him again. He took her in

his arms and she descended in to pleasure once more. As with so

much, she had taught him, and it had been at her suggestion that

their lovemaking had been augmented with the liberal use of

cocaine. Steve hadn't the heart to refuse her, and if truth be told he

had welcomed the chance to experiment and to break out of

convention which had seemed to mark him down as mediocre ever

since he could remember. But here, in the dark, he was anything

but mediocre, with Terry he had found a new lease of life and the

chance to broaden his experience. He reached for her now, and found her warm body beneath the covers and moved closer. Dinner could wait.

Nobody had ever said that it would be like this. Nobody had said anything about the hours, the noise and the mindless repetition. No, this had all been kept nicely under wraps at the interview and it had all come as a glorious surprise on the first day of what Louie had come to regard as his very own personal hell. Somehow, it had all seemed a lot brighter during the recruitment and the induction . Louie had been part of a new batch of recruits, eager to share in the success of the Cherokee, to be a part of something, to be a team player. The work was straightforward and each recruit had been introduced to their cell and quickly made welcome. Volumes had been low initially and there was time to learn about his new work mates , to develop his own skills and to understand the system, and more importantly, the ways to beat it. But now, volume was king, quality was a poor relation and line rates had been massively stepped up. With little investment in high technology, higher volumes were achieved by recruiting more men, by running twenty four hour shifts and by cutting corners and working weekends. It had never been like this in the brochure.

Louie's team had grown from twelve to twenty two men all trying to stay out of the 'hole' and get their job done before the conveyor moved their job beyond reach. Each man had at least three jobs to do, all calculated to the last second and each dependent on the one before. When he had started, each daily target had been 140 units a day, now it was closer to 225 and still they were supposed to hit quality targets. Their only tools were the pneumatic jackhammers that had virtually become a part of each of them as they squirmed between bulkheads, vehicles and each other. They were a team now alright, through necessity. No team member could allow one of his number to fall behind as this would impact on his own job and when all was said and done stopping the line was like signing your own redundancy papers and it was the numbers that mattered, nothing else. They had seen initiatives come and go, young managers with fancy ideas , total quality, just in time, change management, team -building , uniforms and morning exercise. They had seen them all, and through them all they hadn't changed a thing knowing that when the chips were down the only thing that really mattered was to shift metal and shift it fast. But somehow he hadn't thought it would be like this. Maybe that was the problem, he hadn't thought. He, like countless others before him, had been swayed by the prospect of ready cash in his pocket. For the first time in his life he had had the chance to get out from under and he wasn't about to let it pass him by.

Louie had been recruited by Michaels with another recruit named Barnes who had recently joined their team from one further down the line and they had been stationed next to each other. You couldn't help but get to know a man when you are working in his sweat so Barnes and Louie had become a strong team among the assembly line fraternity with one important difference. Like Louie, Barnes had struggled with the monotonous pace, the noise and ever-increasing need to do it better, faster and smarter but he had found a way to adjust . Stevie Barnes was a speed merchant.

When Louie had joined Barnes on the line he had struggled to maintain the pace and he just couldn't work out how Barnes was able to keep on track even to the extent of taking on an extra job to keep them out the hole. Whilst others struggled, Barnes appeared to be choreographed , his actions a blur of applied energy, no wasted time, no wasted effort. The line siders * had quickly learned to keep Stevie Barnes supplied for two good reasons. His temper was legendary, and his section was the basis for all the others further down the line. Barnes had explained it to him. Louie Jameson took his first step up the ladder.

It had been a mistake, a big mistake, he knew that now. But knowing it and solving it were two different things. They needed another patsy and they needed him now. It wasn't a difficult job, to be honest a chimp could do it, but it had to be their chimp. A chimp they could control, a chimp who would ask no questions, tell no lies and get the job done. Michaels had been wrong to lean so heavily on the youngster but as the volumes increased so did the profits.

It had all seemed so simple. The key had been modesty and even now he was surprised how well the plan had progressed. It was simple after all - staggeringly so.

With the ever increasing pressure throughout the United States and Latin America, Western Europe had become the new battleground. Western Europe was to be the new market which would provide the customers of the future, Western Europe would

provide the next generation of consumers for the worlds most

expensive commodity. The cartel had studied the birth of the new

European market and dreamt of untold riches. As each new country

synchronised its tariffs so customs searches became a thing of the

past. As currencies were co-ordinated the cartel had seen massive

new potential among the young and disaffected youth of the

fledgling democracies and began to consider shipments far beyond

the norm. Single couriers would no longer support the volumes that

would be needed to sustain such a market. A way had to be found to

transport large quantities, with minimum risk, high yield and

constant supply. Only then could Western Europe be harvested .

Donnegan had first conceived the plan in the summer of

1998 and he had been amazed that no one had thought of it before.

It had offered all the advantages of continuous supply, low risk,

potentially high yields and short delivery times.

Put all that together with a supply chain that was virtually undetectable and Donnegan believed that he had all the pieces to deliver substantial volumes to the cartel and do himself no small amount of good in to the bargain. As with all good plans it had taken a dedicated team months of planning but in the end it had all been so easy and the 'pipeline' had lain undetected for the last four months.

Like all good businessmen, Donnegan had a perfectly respectable front in the North East. He had been a pillar of the Chamber since its inception and it was in his interests to cultivate his peers which he did with an almost God given zeal. His network had provided valuable leads on more than one occasion and now would be the time for payback. Similarly, there were those who had resisted his approaches, here too, there would be payback, slow, inexorable but payback nonetheless. Donnegan's cartel was obviously not the only game in town but with the 'pipeline' in place all other suppliers were being slowly eased out through a combination of knock down pricing, wide availability, brutal intimidation and ruthless violence. Slowly, the cartel had established a bridgehead, consolidated their position and built outwards. The inner cities had been the obvious place to start and three areas had been targeted specifically, the estates of Mosside, the terraces of Handsworth and the London Docklands. The growth had been slow at first but now expansion had realised a successful joining of the Birmingham and Manchester centres with the M40 providing a rapid transport corridor between the southern and northern corridors. All this had been achieved in a little under six months.

The turning point had been the recruitment of Terry and that prat from the States - Donnegan was even now not sure whether Gaynor had worked out what was going on , but even if he did Donnegan could hang him out to dry anytime he liked.

With Donnegan's contacts being invited to host the US visit had been a formality and the manipulation had been proved easier than he had dared to hope. Terry had had him eating out of her hand before the close of the deal and the extra days had only served to strengthen their synthetic relationship. He would pull her out soon enough, but for the time being the arrangement suited him well enough.

In the meantime, the remaining pieces of the jigsaw had been put in place and the 'pipeline'' had flowed soon after. Recruiting other team members had been easy enough. Each link in the chain knew only enough to carry out his assigned task and no more. In the whole operation there were really only four operations and they were stunning in their simplicity. 'The Plant' had proved to be a rich source of recruits both for this operation and for the others that

Donnegan oversaw, but the 'pipeline" had proved to be his best deal yet.

Street-ready heroin has started flowing at the start of the year and hadn't stopped. 'The Pipeline' ran from the heart of the States to the heart of the United Kingdom, courtesy of General Motors. It was brilliant if he said so himself.

Donnegan had specifically looked at the four operational areas himself. First, there was the construction of the chassis, a complicated operation involving jigs and robotic welding rigs subcontracted to a major chassis manufacturer in downtown Washington where costs were low and security lower. The actual operation was managed by one man.

The second operation was simplicity itself and actually required very little from Donnegan's team. The finished chassis, wax

injected and officially sealed by not insubstantial bumpers was
transported into GM and began its journey to trackside. Donnegan's
only input was to control the scheduling of specific chassis to
specific markets, once again a one-man operation. Once the chassis
had become a complete vehicle it was shipped to the waiting
market where Donnegan's people undertook the pre-delivery
inspection, removed the bumpers, attached the towing gear,
removed the merchandise and shipped it out of the factory in the
scrap bins. Only here had Donnegan cause for worry. More people
were involved, more palms had to be greased, but it still worked.
And the reason why it all worked so well was because each cog in
the machine knew nothing and because each cog was himself
heavily dependent on Donnegan for his job and his habit.

Only once had Donnegan had a problem. The initial chassis
construction had been moved in house and this meant that the
recruitment of somebody new. It hadn't been a huge problem,

Donnegan had Michaels on the shopfloor but the boy Michaels had recommended hadn't proved suitable and had been removed . Consequently Michaels had given him a problem. A link in the chain had been broken - an minor link but a link nonetheless. Without anybody to actually load the merchandise whilst the chassis was being stamped the whole process would grind to a halt and Donnegan had to move fast before somebody was brought in who either couldn't be bought or who didn't have a habit.

The Pipeline (2)

Sean Mason was thirty seven, divorced and cynical. If you wanted to be charitable to him, you would describe him as a craggy six foot one, if you wanted to put the boot in then he had seen his best days and they had not been kind to him. He smoked too much, drank in binges and wouldn't know a decent meal if it introduced itself. He was still reasonably fit, he had little choice when Harry made no effort to stay in trim , but he was finding it harder to lose the pounds and easier to give in to temptation. Temptation - you could say that had been Sean's watchword for the last ten years. He had been tempted to join the DEA from the regular force and he had been tempted into a disastrous marriage which had bled him dry to this day. Sean just thanked God there were no children.

If Sean was honest the move to the DEA had been about the only logical move left to him, he had been passed over twice too often and knew that he was never going to make captain if he had stayed where he was. The move sideways had at least meant new people, new experiences and the chance to work with Harry.

Harry was everything Sean was not. Medium height, medium build, medium marriage. Harry was mediocrity personified and it was because of this that Sean despised him so much. At least Sean had tried to make a decent life. At least Sean hadn't decided twenty years ago that this was all there was ever going to be. At least Sean had had something once, even if it was just a distant memory now.

Harry was fifty three, drove a nondescript saloon and had a nondescript wife Sean had never met. (Hell - they'd only been working together for three years why should he have met his wife ?) Sean had never looked for that kind of support anyway - if he wanted to meet people he could go to his local bar - if truth be told Sean didn't like meeting people - most of the ones he'd met had either tried to kill him or stitch him up. It wasn't a very charitable viewpoint but it was how he felt. Sean did know that Harry had a couple of kids somewhere and that Harry had an apartment on the west side of town. But that was about all he did know and all he cared to find out.

Sean looked across at him now ,as they waited for the plant personnel officer. Despite everything, Sean guessed Harry must have had something going for him , or else why had they stayed together for so long?

"Lost anybody recently ? "

Sean knew that it was a cheap crack but conversational niceties
had never been his style and he wasn't about to change now. Sean
also knew that with the absenteeism which was virtually endemic in
any big plant these guys wouldn't miss anybody until the statutory
period of sick leave had been exceeded by some days.
" Its hard to say, (God it was so predictable), with the shift patterns
we work here its hard for us to keep regular records for all our
associates (Associates ! For Chrissakes who did these people think
they were kidding ?) "
The personnel officer had introduced himself as George Masters
and Sean had to admit that if you took away the suit-speak he was
probably a half-decent guy. Harry was talking to him now,
"How soon will you know ? We've got photographs, can we talk to
your people and get an id?",

Masters was looking a little uncomfortable now. The last thing he needed was a public drugs scandal during the selling season. He knew drugs were finding their way into the plant and he probably had a good idea who was responsible, but it just wasn't worth the effort to close it down , only to have it return somewhere else, under new control. Having said that he could hardly condone drug abuse on his site. The papers would have a field day and his arse would be in a sling for months.

"If you give me the picture, I should be able to get a positive identification before close of play".

Masters had decided to play ball, he couldn't stand in their way and to do so was just going to prolong the inevitable.

"Leave me a number and I'll ring you before six"

(There, that hadn't been too painful, had it)

Harry was talking again,

"If he is one of yours, we'll need to talk to some of his work mates, if that's okay ?"

It was an obvious question , but like I said , Harry was a stickler for

procedure. In his own mind Sean had already filed this case under

'Unfortunate consequences of society breakdown' and the sooner

he could put the whole thing away , the better.

"If you can let me know, when you would like to start, that would

be fine" ,

Masters was back on solid ground now. So long as he could control

what happened he figured that he could contain any negative

publicity that might arise. Harry was getting up, his business

seemingly finished, Masters had started something new on his

desk , it appeared that this audience was over. Sean checked out

the office as he moved towards the door. It was nothing special.

The corporate colours were obviously grey and blue as they

decorated everything from the desks themselves, all the stationery,

the furniture and the pictures which hung round the room,

boasting of some success in some far-distant corner of the globe.

God help you if you didn't like grey and blue.

Michaels was not looking forward to this particular week. Personnel had informed him , (Personnel never just told anybody anything) that his team was below par and that unless Nicky Jenkins turned up for work that week, then either his teams must be rearranged or a new recruit would have to be found. Donnegan had told him something similar with the subtle difference that both he and Donnegan knew that Nicky Jenkins was never going to come back to work, or anywhere else.

Michaels hadn't enjoyed watching the boy die, but it had been necessary. He had too much time and money invested in this, to see it all fail now. He was up to his neck in it, and he knew it. Up to now Donnegan had shown himself to be a reasonable man and they had worked well together. He didn't know the whole story but he knew enough to take Donnegan with him and he knew that without a new recruit on the chassis line the whole scheme would die. Whilst he enjoyed the sense of power this information gave him, he also realised that he needed Donnegan much more than Donnegan needed him.

Michaels was not overly concerned, drug abuse among the associates was not uncommon, he just needed to find a user who wasn't too greedy.

For Michaels himself, Donnegan's scheme had been particularly timely. Michaels had succumbed to the twin scourges of the male gender, a wife with expensive taste and a love-hate relationship with the horses. He loved them, they hated him. For Michaels the arrangement was simple, turn a blind eye to what was going into the chassis and make sure the 'associate' responsible had a habit. Considering that half the 'associates' working in the plant had a habit, the last condition had not been too difficult to fulfil. As long as his section wasn't responsible for any major line stoppages and his scrap rate was within tolerances then he was generally left to run his own show. Sure, there was always the abuse from managers looking for a scapegoat for some new initiative which hadn't worked, but he could handle that. His part in Donnegan's pipeline

had so far paid for a holiday in Majorca, a mink for Paula and more

donkeys than Michaels cared to remember.

The Cherokee was the best dual purpose off-road vehicle in the

world and competed not only with the normal run-of-the-mill

offerings from Japan but also numbered luxury executive saloons

amongst its competitors. It retailed for close to fifty thousand

pounds which although not expensive , did push it beyond the likes

of Michaels and his team. Its off road ability had been threatened

many times, but the engineers had always come up with some

gizmo and the pricing guys had just moved it into the stratosphere.

In truth, the Cherokee was particularly well suited to Donnegan's

pipeline, it was one of the few cars still built with a separate chassis

, something that had long since disappeared on its more mundane brethren, and it was sufficiently hand-built to cover the weight discrepancy that the 'pipeline' bestowed upon it. Its method of construction was simple. The chassis was built as two interlocking 'U' shaped members forming an enclosed ladder of immense strength. The chassis thus provided all the anchor points for the suspension, drivetrain, heating and cooling systems, a safe location for the wiring loom and the perfect location for drug smuggling.

Once the bumpers had been fitted in Michaels section the chassis progressed down the line where it eventually met the body structure monocoque, a cage-like framework of extruded steel which ultimately housed the occupants of the vehicle and which was securely bolted to the chassis in ten locations.

The biggest obstacle for Donnegan was not getting the drugs out but getting them in, in the first place. Although the plant was totally designed to take parts and sub-assemblies from suppliers all over the world and thus the perfect site to simply add another supplier, the administration and control necessary had meant that this area of the pipeline had the largest headcount and as a simple result of that , the greatest possibility of error. In reality, it had been the work of a couple of minutes to set up an additional part number from an established supplier and schedule delivery to Michaels section , but the work of many weeks had secured this supplier as a bona fide parts supplier who had recently achieved the highest quality standards and whose real parts were amongst the best in the business. Making an additional delivery to Michaels' section had easily been arranged and once Donnegan had hit upon the idea to mould the resin to match exactly the packing used to secure the rear axle in transit the plan had appeared foolproof. This 'packing' was simply stacked as the axles became part of the vehicle but instead of being returned to the supplier it was simply incorporated in to the build process itself, sealed behind the bumpers until it was recovered at journeys end. In The North East it was simply unloaded and returned to a bogus supplier and distributed by Donnegan's growing network of dealers and pushers.

When the vehicle was complete ,which usually took a day, it was tested and scheduled for shipping. Three days later it would be transported to the dockside, driven into the hold to emerge three weeks later for a final pre-delivery inspection, when the protective wax was removed, the bumpers removed to ease the fitment of the towing equipment, the drugs removed and the vehicle sent on its way.

It was of course a supreme irony ,that had not been lost on Donnegan, that many of the vehicles that Donnegan scheduled to support his pipeline were usually ordered by the very people Donnegan was putting out of business.

Stevie had known that it was only a matter of time before the police would want to talk to him. He had known what was going on in Michaels section for some time. He had seen a succession of new recruits come and go and he had seen Michaels weld a team out of a bunch of no-hopers, crack heads and misfits. His role was always the same, take them under his wing, show them the ropes and educate them to the ways of Michaels' world. Most of the time the recruits realised what Michaels' section was all about fairly quickly and either moved on or carved themselves a niche, supplying, using or just being plain bloody minded.

Jenkins had been different, if only in his naivety. Jenkins had launched into his new 'career' (his words) on the line with all the zeal that his tender years could conjure up. The heavy duty world of industry had appeared as some new playground and Jenkins had been blind to the more profitable aspects of Michaels operation. In Stevie's opinion ,Michaels had seriously misjudged Jenkins when he had first introduced him to the joys of the chassis line. Jenkins, had seen the potential immediately, not for the long term benefits, but for the short term leverage he could bring to bear on Michaels. It had been a bad idea, which could only end one way. Stevie knew Michaels had killed Jenkins, or had him killed (what was the difference ?). Stevie knew how Michaels worked and it wasn't pleasant. He knew that the police would show up, he knew they would want to talk to him and he knew Michaels needed a new patsy.

-

Stevie looked around him now, above the lines offices had been arranged to house the massed banks of computer screens that seemed to be the font of all knowledge and to give the 'gaffers' somewhere to handle the more formal of their tasks. Stevie guessed that interviewing a possible murder suspect was a formal task.

"How well did you know Nicky Jenkins ?"

Sean still couldn't see the investigation going anywhere but with

Harry, nothing was ever left unresolved.

"As well as you can get know anybody in this cage, he was okay"

"How come he ended up in a dumpster then?"

Sean and Harry hadn't planned how they were going to interview

Jenkins' workmates, and it showed. It usually turned into some sort

of good cop, bad cop routine but today wasn't one of their better

days. Today it was just two bad cops.

"Look, you do your hours, you take your pay, you keep your nose

clean, you go home. Its not a big deal. You know how it works. You

don't know anything, you weren't here when it happened, you've

never seen the guy before.

"So what can you tell us ?"

"Jesus, are you guys for real ? You don't listen and you don't

understand .Do you really think I'm ready to spill my guts because

I'm a good citizen. You don't have any idea what this is all about do you"

"Suppose you tell us"

"Suppose you find yourself another patsy"

Sean had heard it a thousand times before. It was the reason behind the whole charade. 'People had a right to know', people had a right not to get involved' . Just so long as it didn't cross into my backyard everything in the garden was rosy - Sean hated them all. What had happened to everybody taking responsibility for each other - Sean wondered, not for the first time, what the hell he was doing here.

"How's the job"

Harry was probing now, looking for an angle.

"The jobs fine. Look, you know the score, the job's shit, so you do a little dope, sometimes the kids take it a little too far. What do you want me to say ? I'm not his dad."

"Who else knew him ?" Harry continued to press.

"Michaels recruited him, I guess he must know him"

Sean could see Harry was getting nowhere, Stevie Barnes had the disaffected grown up kid routine down pat and he wasn't shaken by Harry's attempts to shift him out of his complacency. Rule number one, look after number one.

If Harry and Sean were honest the investigation wasn't moving too fast. So far they had nothing to go on except the company uniform and a standard needle set that could be exchanged at any one of a hundred exchange centres across the city. There were no witnesses, no finger prints, no tyre tracks, no distinguishing marks or dodgy clothing. Why was it never like this in the movies ? From the residue in the syringe Sean knew that what Jenkins had injected would have had half of Manhattan partying till Thanksgiving , what he didn't know was whether it was deliberate or whether someone wanted him put away. The level of overdose suggested that either Jenkins was new to the game or he was deliberately killed. The long lines of puncture marks along his forearms suggested this wasn't his debut

so Sean had come to the logical conclusion that somebody wanted

him silenced. It was information but it has hardly conclusive

evidence.

Sean and Harry were trying to find out anything about the boy, but

in a city of seven million where everybody kept themselves to

themselves and nobody sees anything this was not as easy as it

sounded. Jenkins had moved to the Washington area after a

succession of jobs hoping to get a job at the 'plant'. He was

originally from Cleveland, had an elderly mother still there (who

would have to be told) and was not exactly the brightest thing to

come out of Cleveland (Sean couldn't even hazard a guess at that

one), and wouldn't be missed by anybody. (Michaels had chosen

well). Jenkins had an apartment towards the centre of town. It

would be their next stop.

Sean was not exactly new to the delights of single male living, His own apartment wasn't exactly "Homes & Gardens" but compared to what they found at 223 Upper Freemont, Sean was living in a palace.

Upper Freemont had seen better days. The streets had once been wide boulevards, the houses had once been showpieces but the wealth which had created them had moved on out to the suburbs and they were now nothing more than shells hiding a thousand sad bedsits and forlorn dreams. The debris of a failing urban fabric was all too obvious. On the streets what cars there were, were bricked up shells stripped of all value and simply awaiting the next cold snap. Gardens which had once vied for attention now stood in sad decay, struggling to survive amongst the contamination of bricks, corrugated steel, oil drums and car parts that cluttered what little space there was. Children played in pools of foul smelling effluent whilst torn posters encouraged the residents to join up with the 'Democratic Crusade Against Poverty' or to 'Take a Course and

Make A Brighter Tomorrow'. Sean knew that nothing short of mass revolution could make a better tomorrow here, and if things got much worse that was a distinct possibility.

Sean and Harry worked their way across the street and found their way to 223 - it wasn't the worst but that wasn't saying much. The tenement building was five storeys, four of which appeared to be empty, the top floor was still occupied, but no. 223 had clearly not been used for some time. The halls were decorated with drunks sleeping it off, a variety of graffiti, yet more debris and an assortment of bottles which indicated that the delights of designer beers had yet to reach this neighbourhood.

Inside the story was the same. The rooms had once been quite spacious but now the space had been corralled into what Sean knew were euphemistically called 'individual living units' . To Sean , all that meant was a bunch of bedsits with peeling paper, damp rising out of the lino and the usual clapped out furniture and excuses for home comforts. Nicky Jenkins may have had a new

'career' at 'the plant' but whatever he was bringing home wasn't

being spent on nest-building. Judging from the surroundings Sean

wasn't even sure Jenkins had actually moved in - only the more

recent rubbish gave any indication that the room had been

occupied in the recent past. This wasn't The Village. (No shit,

Sherlock).

Bedsits were soul-destroying places at the best of times but this

one could have broken hearts for England. The front door (Sean

couldn't think what else to call it) was no more than two sheets of

hardboard roughly painted a rather fetching shade of puce but

somehow the paint hadn't got the stomach to cover some of the

more unseemly stains that even now discoloured the door and the

boards beneath. The room itself continued the theme and Sean was

sure that no doubt somewhere in the upmarket suburbs of Queens

there were people desperate to recreate the distressed urban look -

no matter what they spent they were never going to get close to this.

Tacked to the inside of the door were a selection of faded notices imploring residents not to smoke, not to make noise, not to have guests (forget about enjoying yourself in here guys) and a further selection reminding all those that entered that hot water was a precious commodity, that the rubbish was cleared on a Thursday, that taxis were available from "A.F.O." and that Mandy would provide discrete personal services all for the price of a phone call to her customer friendly '0898' number. Sean wasn't sure where the rubbish was cleared to - to him it looked as though it was just dumped straight down the stairs.

The green theme was continued into the room but somehow Sean thought green had been a poor choice. The carpet, such as it was, was threadbare so, at one time this room had had considerable traffic or else it had just been there one helluva long time. Once it might have had a discernible design but now it was just mush which blended seemlessly with the mush growing up from the walls and sprouting from behind the sink in the furthest corner of the room. Sean tried to be positive, at least the room had a window, the bed looked clean (although he wasn't about to spend a night in it) and the aircon unit thrumming in the corner at least made the temperature bearable. But that was it. Even Harry appeared shocked.

"What the hell are we looking for?"

Harry knew damn well what they were looking for and he also knew that Sean didn't really give a damn and had already decided that the bedsit would not reveal anything of value.

"Lets just give it a quick look then get out of here, okay"

For once Harry didn't give him an argument. For once the process would be short.

Louie couldn't believe his job had become so simple. The everyday panic had been replaced with an overwhelming belief that all would be fine and that he could do any of the jobs in the section without having to try. The days of disappearing 'down the hole' were just a dim and distant memory, in fact Louie was having trouble believing it had ever happened. Surely, that had been somewhere else, someone else, sometime never. What did he care. Michaels had got off his back, the section was running like a Swiss watch (he guessed that was good) and his take-home had improved dramatically. Maybe he'd got it wrong. Maybe the brochures had been right after all.

It was dark already. Start in the dark, go home in the dark. The ever-increasing pace of the line had finally switched into virtual 24 hour operation. In truth, Louie knew that the night shift really did no more than put right the cars they had built during the day. When Louie thought that some poor bastard had spent $40,000 on the vehicle in front of him he just thanked God he hadn't got $40,000 of his own. Christ $40,000 , he'd be happy with $400. Stevie was next to him now, working in his sweat, the two of them working without communication but working with almost religious fervour and trance-like efficiency. Louie had finally really joined Michaels team about three weeks before and now it was amazing just how much you could get done in a shift. Without a word and almost as part of the assembly operation a small foil packet dropped into Louie's palm. It was the late shift pick me up. Tea breaks had never been like this at Ford.

Michaels couldn't wait any longer. The pressure from Donnegan had been building for the last few weeks and Michaels knew that Donnegan couldn't afford to have the pipeline disconnected any longer. Christ, with the number of donkeys that he had backed recently, he couldn't afford it any more than Donnegan could. The section was running smoothly and Stevie had done a good job with Louie. He would have to be compromised and brought into the fold.

The date for the pipeline restart had been set for two weeks from now , September 14th, and naturally coincided with the launch of 1999MY. The plant would be in chaos with new parts coming in and old parts being used and shipped out. According to the new doctrines of TQI and JIT the transition between new and old models would be seamless but Michaels had been around too long to be suckered by management bullshit. He knew, as did everybody else that the concept of 'Friday Cars' was alive and well and living in the car industry. He also knew that they were even more prevalent during the model year changeover. He'd seen cars built up from both specifications, he'd seen trim colour changes so subtle that telling them apart in the low light of the assembly line produced cars with two tone interiors and he'd seen heavy duty machinery brought up at trackside to modify parts because some bright spark hadn't remembered that some poor bastard had to fit the damn thing. The model year changeover was the perfect opportunity to restart the pipeline, to bring Louie into the fold and to get back into favour with Donnegan.

In truth , the 'bright sparks' upstairs had made Michaels life easier with the launch of the new model. With new suspension mounting points and improved performance the rear chassis rails had been beefed up and now provided greater space for Donnegan's additional packages. Surely, it couldn't be this simple.

Looking down from the gantries above the line Michaels surveyed his turf, the line running faultlessly beneath him. He could see his men writhing in and out of the cars, the vehicles an almost unrecognisable mass of airlines, parts waiting to be fitted and the men who would have to fit them. Michaels gave thanks everyday that his days on the track, were behind him. Nothing would ever tempt him back.

He saw the transfer between Stevie and Louie as he had watched the transfer between Stevie and Jenkins although he tried not to think about Jenkins these days. It was strange, a year ago Michaels would never have believed that his personal code would sanction the death of another human. But then did he really consider Jenkins as a fellow human or did he really see him as some Neolithic automaton paid to do a job that no self respecting robot would even consider? Michaels had not even been troubled over the boys death. Naturally, he hadn't done it himself, but he had been there. He had known of the party and he had watched as Jenkins had stepped up his drinking before his men had helped him into a car and delivered the fatal dose in the backstreets of downtown Washington. Michaels knew he was clean. The car had been a rental, the men had already been compromised themselves and there was nothing to link them to him. Clean.

The team brief had been one of the more successful management initiatives and had actually survived for two years since its introduction although why it took a management initiative to realise that letting people know what the hell was going on was a good idea was lost on Louie. As far as he was concerned that was a

real no-brainer. He remembered the early days at Ford, when

orders would be taken for all manner of specifications and

somehow the line had to deliver. Forget about model

rationalisation, just take the orders and get it out the gates. At least

here, there was some notice of strange specifications although that

still didn't make it any easier to put the damn things together.

The team brief was Michaels responsibility and Louie listened now

as the new job assignments were announced. He didn't really care

where he went, so long as he stayed on Michaels section and had

Stevie to support him. He knew he would be moving. He had made

it clear that he was keen to help support the section and that meant

ultimately being able to do all the assignments in the section. For

Michaels it meant flexible, reliable labour. For Louie it meant the

chance to move up and make some serious money. He had come to

realise that there were two types of men on the line - those that

just wanted to do their own job for the duration and those that wanted to progress through all the jobs. He couldn't understand

how any man could do the same thing for ten hours a day, six days

a week for fifteen years but it wasn't his problem. Rule number one,

look after number one.

The assignments for the week were sorted, Louie and Stevie were

still together. Louie was beginning to realise that they were

becoming important to Michaels. He just wasn't sure whether that

was good or bad.

Sure enough, Stevie was coming with him , but the choice of

assignment was a little curious as the chassis stamping area was

hardly under serious pressure and yet Michaels had transferred

them both to stamp the rails and fix the bumpers. The process was

virtually stand alone and could be relied upon to never take the

team 'down the hole'. Still, Michaels was the boss and presumably

he knew what he was doing. Although these days that was no

guarantee.

The forensic reports had started to filter back to Sean and Harry

and as Sean had predicted showed little to give them direction.

Nicky Jenkins had died from a massive overdose of heroin. He had

died about two hours before anybody had found him (which was

hardly surprising in that neighbourhood) . His work overalls were

standard issue to over 46000 workers spead over four plants and

his body had shown signs of high alcohol intake prior to the fatal

overdose. His body was beginning to show signs of malnutrition, his

dental work was not exactly up-to-date and the pathologist had

noted a number of cuts and bruises that he had put down to the

day to day rigours of the bodyline. His clothing had shown up a

number of additional fibres which were in widespread use in the

auto industry .In short, nothing spectacular, nothing that was going

to solve the case for them.

The Pipeline: (3)

Louie didn't really care- chassis stamping, axle assembly it was all the same to him. The 'tea breaks' here meant that he could handle anything and he had finally begun to see the light at the end of the tunnel and for the first time in his life it might just take him someplace he did want to go. His partnership with Stevie Barnes had made them a respected part of Michaels' team and they had developed a friendship beyond the need to work in each others shadow. There were few secrets on the chassis line, the nature of the work dictated some way had to be found to keep the mechanics moving smoothly and for Louie and Steve their way had become the norm for the chassis line. For Stevie it meant a nice sideline in soft drugs and yet more respect and by association Louie had become part of the team. The brochures had never said anything about this but he guessed he should have realised and embraced the obvious a helluva lot earlier.

Louie reached briefly to his left and as if by magic the packet was in his hand momentarily, but this time Louie felt uneasy. He looked around furtively, nothing seemed out of place. The line was as it always was, Michaels was in deep conversation at the engine mount section (and Louie knew that Michaels' was at least onside) but it was Donnegan that caused him to start. The production manager was even now striding down the catwalk above the line making for the top of the section with a face that said everything Louie needed to know. Louie had never met Donnegan before and these weren't exactly the circumstances he would have chosen to boost his career prospects. Donnegan grabbed Michaels as he passed him, rudely finishing his conversation and immediately accusing him with gestures and pulling him towards where Louie and Stevie waited, all thoughts of the line forgotten.

Donnegan's office above the line was like any other in the assembly

area. Perched high above the line it gave an unrestricted view of

Donnegan's kingdom and Louie could understand immediately how

easy it had been for Donnegan to see the unscheduled parts

deliveries that Stevie had orchestrated from their section.

Louie Jameson knew what a good chewing out looked and felt like

and he had to admit that Donnegan was a master. He had started

with Michaels, then driven seemlessly into Stevie systematically

stripping away any veneer of management professionalism and

descending into the language of the backstreets which made his

feelings very clear indeed. Only in the punishment did Donnegan

revert to management protocal leaving Michaels the onerous task

of completing the personnel formalities, the official warnings and

what Jameson knew would finally come down to dismissal. No time

was given for this second meeting with Michaels. For the time being

Stevie and Jameson were to be left to finish their shift and contemplate their futures on welfare.

Stevie Barnes had long since ceased to be impressed by Donnegan's charade but he had to admit to anybody looking on from the outside it did look like a dramatic dressing down which would only help to reinforce his position of authority on the shopfloor. Even Stevie knew that Donnegan was virtually a deity to those that worked for him. Donnegan's history was chassis line folklore. He had been with the company all his working life, starting on the production floor which had now become his kingdom. He had had to move out of the company twice to get the moves he had wanted but he had always been brought back to the line which he had made his own . He had had stints at Ford and Chrysler but the Cherokee had always been his. He had risen quickly to become the youngest production manager the company had ever had and unlike some of his contemporaries he had continued his rise to director equally quickly. Along the way he had lost two wives and there had been rumours of affairs and crippling alimony. It all just

added to the mystique.

For Louie Jameson the reasons behind his move to the stamping

area and his recent dressing down became all to clear as the first

1995 MY cars started down the track. Michaels had made it very

clear that he now owned every aspect of his life and only when

Jameson had had this fully explained to him with the aid of some

judicial physical persuasion had Michaels explained the real role of

the chassis stamping area. Louie had been given his choices, Stevie

had been given his cut - Michaels had his patsy. Business as usual.

Louie Jameson had never been what you might call a hardened

criminal. He had cruised on the fringes since his early teens but had

so far managed to avoid anything really serious although this had

always had more to do with being in the wrong place at the right time rather than any real intention on Louie's part. Recreational crime was how Louie came to consider it , at least subconsciously. Some people played soccer, some went to the gym, some played the horses, Louie played the odds against getting caught. It had long ceased to be a challenge . The pathetic level of security on your average condo had often reduced Louie to silent laughter but it was a hobby that had held his interest longer than most and morality was not exactly his strong suit. Sure, 'the plant' had provided some security and to be honest his recruitment into Michaels' operation had come as a welcome distraction, but putting resin impregnated packing into Cherokee bumpers wasn't exactly brain surgery, now was it. The shift pattern whilst not exactly conducive to a happy home life did not impinge on Louie's nocturnal activities and now that he had truly joined the Michaels' operation the work wasn't going to kill him. He could stamp chassis in his sleep , and frequently did.

He was not what you would call conventional. His parents had given

up the idea of responsible parenting about the same time as Louie

had discovered girls, cars and crime (even now Louie had trouble

deciding which gave him most pleasure) and from then at least the

crime had never looked back. The girls had varied but there had

never been anything close to a period of celibacy and cars had

always been there although Louie had to admit that he had yet to

really scale the heights in that department. The Cherokee was nice

but Louie could take it apart with his eyes closed (who couldn't ?)

and as far as he was concerned it still had some way to go to

compare with a three pointed star or anything that came out of

Munich. He didn't mind putting it together but he sure as shit

wasn't going to buy one.

The condo was dark. There was some light from the back but it was

set back from the road but Louie had never been one to concern

himself with the niceties of his hobby. Home, not home, he really didn't care - it was just another job . The french windows were a joke. What was the point of fitting seven locks when the glass was this easy to push out ? The beading levered off with a screwdriver and Louie lowered the pane of glass to the ground. It hadn't taken more than a minute. The french windows opened out onto a large sitting room , deep soft furnishings and dark wood. The deep lustre of brass contrasted with mahogany and ebony, the floor was awash with deep pile carpeting. Off to the left the room opened out into a second room dominated by a dark table and eight chairs. One wall was covered in an assortment of photographs whilst at the angle the mood changed dramatically with several deep abstract paintings conjuring up images from the four corners of the world. Louie had no idea where the four corners of the world were, his experience was strictly limited to the four corners of Washington's west side and that was none too savoury.

Sean and Harry were getting nowhere and they weren't even doing it fast. The death of Nick Jenkins was not exactly high on their priority list. It was either a clumsy hit or a clumsy junkie - who really cared ? The 'plant' had thrown up a number of people that even Sean considered distasteful but it was hardly proof in a homicide investigation. After the initial burst of co-operation, the suits had submerged Sean and Harry with an ever increasing bureaucracy and mounds of paper proving how clean their plant was and Sean knew that he was being steered towards closing the file. Comments had been made, 'donations' received and Sean wanted to move on. Where was the harm ?

There were no witnesses. The clothing went nowhere. There were no prints. Deadend. Leave it . Close the book, it would be so easy. Who would care ?.

Harry, bloody Harry would care. Harry - the bloody process, always the bloody process. For once, Sean had had to concede that Harry's concentration on process was a sight to see. He was like a dog with

a bone, he just couldn't put it down. Where the hell did he get off ?

He had worked systematically tracking down those who had been

allowed to get close to Nicky Jenkins. They had been few and even

among them Nicky was still a closed book. He had come down from

Cleveland, drawn by the glitter of the city, all he had found was a

dead-end job - which in this case had proved sadly prophetic. His

downcast apartment had revealed a downcast life enlightened,

when cash had allowed by the twin popular opiates of drink and

drugs. None of Nicky's contemporaries were overly surprised by his

death. They seemed more concerned with the lengths that Harry

was going to over what was nothing more than everyday urban

wallpaper.

Sean and Harry both knew they had little option. The simple

information was drying up, what they needed was someone on the

inside. It was always dangerous but Sean had little choice. Only

Stevie Barnes had actually been involved up to now and Harry had done the majority of the talking there. Sean's problem was with authority (no change there) . If he involved the suits at the precinct or those at 'the plant' there were too many snouts in the trough. Too many things that could go wrong. Sean had seen what could happen to somebody on the wrong end of a steel press and it wasn't pretty. With the number of donations that had been received recently some pretty heavy duty pressure was being brought to bear. Sean should close the book but for once he wasn't about to, just because it was what was expected. Sean was never good with what he was supposed to do. 'The plant' was recruiting, he should be able to pass the entrance exams but he had to be sure he would be allocated the right assignment. Masters would have to be brought onside. God knows how he would react to having the DEA on his turf. (Tough).

Sean had never even seen the brochures but he knew now that going undercover was about as bright a move as he had ever made.

How he had ever believed he could handle the sheer physical

endurance was now beyond him. He had never known anything like

this and he was sure his physical failings were starting to

compromise his position in the team. This was like no team Sean

had ever been on. It was based on one overriding principle, physical

presence, physical respect and total mutual dependency. Sean was

finding out the hard way all the truths that had dogged Louie in the

early days only he was doing it without the support of Stevie Barnes

or his regular pick me ups.

Masters had come round eventually but that had just been the

start. Michaels had balked at the introduction of a new 'face' and

the close knit-team was starting to take against him. Michaels had

gone out of his way to challenge Sean with the worst sections and

the most demanding work all done at a pace that Sean had found

awe-inspiring from the outside and deeply intimidating from the

inside. He was spending a lot of the time 'down the hole' and the

support of those around him was taking longer to happen and no longer came without comment or abuse. Michaels was conspicuous by his absence and Sean had learned the thick end of sod all for all his efforts over the last two weeks. His time in 'the plant' was dictated by the continual, non-stop pace of the 'track' which never stopped, whilst his inability to handle the pace was now compromising his ability to gain any knowledge outside of work hours with fellow workers who resented his soft hands, slow pace and the effect he was having on their volume and quality bonuses. There weren't many teams that could survive the loss of cold hard cash and this was one was no exemption. Put all that together with Sean's complete inability to provide Harry with anything meaningful meant the whole operation could be compromised or cancelled anytime soon. (It just got better and better didn't it !)

In truth, Sean had little option but to continue the charade. To pull out now would alert Michaels and put his own and Masters' lives on the line. He had no other leads to follow up so either he stuck it out or simply put the file at the back of the drawer. It wouldn't be closed but he sure as shit wouldn't be opening it again.

Sean knew drugs were highly visible in the section but this was hardly unusual and proved nothing. Nobody was kicking and screaming over it and to be honest Sean had considered reverting to a forgotten habit and joining the team if it would make life easier. (Hell, anything that made life easier was worth a try at the moment) . In the two weeks since his recruitment Sean had built two and a half thousand cars, it felt like two and a half million. He had had his eyes opened. He may have achieved his volume target but he sure as well wasn't going to buy a Cherokee anytime soon. His working environment was defined by the length of his air hose. In effect he was confined to a piece of ground eight foot square. He could reach across the track and he could talk to four other 'associates'. None of them had known Nicky Jenkins and all had been recruited from other sections within the last two weeks. (Convenient).

The only time Sean got out of his own section was when he went 'down the hole' when he had to disconnect his airgun, and reconnect it further down the line, effectively disrupting two sections and compromising quality and volume still further.

Outside his life may have been shit, but it was better than this.

He had little opportunity to develop his meagre skills. Michaels had kept him with the same men and in the same section throughout so his knowledge of other processes was negligible and Michaels had been very keen to make sure he got little opportunity to talk to anybody who had known the late, great Nicky Jenkins. (Going well, wasn't it)

Sean's only break from the monotony had come two days previously when a chassis had been thrown off the track as its exhaust had snagged and turned over half a ton of steel like some child's toy. All hell had broken loose with 'gaffers' coming from all directions whilst the majority of the men cheered emphatically and took the opportunity for a smoke, nothing summed up the difference between then and us more clearly for Sean. The distraction had been all the more welcome as it had coincided with the Press Launch of 1999 MY. 'The Plant' had been crawling with the scribbling masses eager to savour the latest incarnation and to swallow the management hype surrounding it. Sean could only guess that the launch had included guided tours of the factory floor as production had been awash with 'guests' for the last week and that day had been no exemption. (God, its just so predictable) Sean had to laugh ;on the day of the stoppage (Last Thursday - was that when it had happened ? Jesus - what bloody day was it ?) the atmosphere on the track was enlivened by a significant number of female journalists which had brought the line to a standstill.   Never mind the nineties, this place was still firmly stuck in the Seventies. Outside the world had moved on but within the stark confines of the chassis line only the names had changed.

At their last evening meeting Sean had even admitted to Harry that he was getting nowhere fast but Harry was keen to continue the undercover operation and if Sean was honest with himself (now, that would be a new one) Harry had only put into words what he had known all along. Harry's own digging had continued to meet a combination of high level pressure and low level co-operation. Masters had started to lean on the department on the basis that there was no new evidence (new evidence ? - there was no evidence period) to link 'the plant' to the killing so maybe Sean and Harry could go and play somewhere else. All they had to show for their efforts was a wall chart rapidly filling up with question marks and Sean's undisputed failings as an 'associate'. Frankly, it didn't look good. (No shit, Sherlock!)

It was dark, very dark. If there was one thing that Louie was an expert on besides wine women and song or in his case; crime, women and cars, it was the dark. This was the best. An opaque, inky blackness that muffled footsteps and provided thick shadows and blanket silence. No moon. Piece of cake.

Louie stretched into his pocket and the long screw driver took up its customary position. The beading fell away easily and Louie lifted the glass noiselessly. The handle mechanism was just inside and came up easily under his gloved hand. No alarms, no sensors, no problem. Louie stepped in and closed the door behind him. The room was classic new money, Bang & Olufsen, distressed woodwork, leather and more leather. Did anybody ever sit on the stuff ? Louie liked it little and cared less. Simple, portable and expensive were his watchwords. Nouveau chic didn't put cash in his pocket.

Louie padded out of the room and began to climb the stairs. From what he assumed to be the den he could here the muted moans of passion, somehow he doubted he would be disturbed.

The house was larger than Louie normally tackled and represented his first move onto new turf. His local neighbourhood was strictly limited in its ability to provide quality merchandise and to be fair

the thrill of the chase was hardly worth it when it proved so easy to

find his fix. He had hoped for a greater challenge but thusfar even

here it was a breeze. The door to the master bedroom was partially

open, Louie glimpsed what he considered to be some pretty tacky

furniture and acres of bedsheets (now those, he may find a use

for). The dressing-table was covered in potions and perfumes but

as ever the jewellery was in the top drawer. Louie took the box, he

would check it later but doubted there would be much paste.

'What the hell are you doing ?!'

Louie whirled, in the doorway stood a man dressed only in shorts

who appeared to be struggling to come to terms with the facts in

front of him. Louie didn't need asking twice. He flew at the door

knocking the guy aside who tumbled untidily towards the floor. The

wide open spaces downstairs were now calling to Louie as if he had

been away for a long time (which was exactly what would happen

unless he got out fast)   but the stoned guy was not quite finished yet and mustered what were left of his faculties and sent Louie

falling with a simple heel tap. (Surely, it wasn't all going to end here

?) Quickly, Louie got to his feet and crashed the jewel box into the

face in front of him. He heard the bone break and judging by the

blood this guy was never going to make a comeback on the catwalk.

Impatient now, Louie rushed for the stairs where he was stopped in

his tracks by two sights which even now were sending sharply

contrasting messages to a brain that was fast reaching overload.

The first was a tall, slim figure partially dressed in flowing silk. The

gown was failing miserably in its attempts to disguise the figure

beneath and Louie was already filling in the missing bits. Dusky

nipples contrasting with deeply tanned skin peaked from beneath

diaphanous folds. The breasts were small but exquisitely pert, the

stomach flat and the mons pubis a perfect triangle of tailored, crisp

hair. The legs were long and strong and stood now braced against

the potential recoil of what looked to Louie like a very nasty

shooter indeed. This most definitely was not in the plan. Even Louie didn't mess with the business end of shooters. Both arms were locked, framing the perfect breasts, the legs slightly apart . Louie could only now bring himself to raise his gaze to the face above.

Brown eyes, a shock of blonde hair. The eyes made it pretty clear, this lady meant business.

'Get up, slowly. Get your hands on your head' .

The voice was calm and clear. If anything she was in a better state than he was. Louie stood and raised his hands above his head. His brain was still not reacting to anything close to logical thought and to be honest the vision in front of him was not helping one little bit. She held all the aces. For the moment he would just have to play his cards and see what happened. Judging by the state of the boyfriend a call to the boys in blue was only going to cause more problems than it was going to solve. But Louie had no idea what Plan B was. He was still struggling with Plan A.

She started to relax and pulled the gown closer to her. For once Louie was actually pleased as at least now he could focus on the job in hand. They were at the top of the stairs, the jewel box was open on the floor. Louie had no idea where the nearest phone was. Now that she had the upper hand, she appeared at a loss. It occurred to Louie that the tidiest way out of this would be for her to blow his brains all over the carpet. No nasty questions, no interrogation, nice and simple perpetrator caught in the act. She would have plenty of time to sober up the boyfriend, agree a story and call the cops. If he'd had the gun, that's the way he'd go.

Suddenly, she appeared to come to a decision and began to shepherd Louie towards the stairs. His first chance had gone and he had hardly recognised it.

'Its not too late to party some more'.

Louie tried to se if there were any other possibilities beyond the obvious.

'You have got to be joking ! I wouldn't waste the coke'

Louie guessed that was a 'no' but pressed on anyway, he hadn't exactly got a lot to lose.

'Come on baby, this could still be a result, what d'ya say ?'

'I say, shut your fat mouth ! '

The point was clear and backed up with a sharp poke to his ribs. It was the chance he had been waiting for. For the second time that night he whirled and grabbed at the pistol, forcing it away from him and twisting the handle brutally in the woman's hand. She was forced to clear the trigger guard or risk having her finger broken. At the same time his free hand punched hard into her stomach. It was hardly fair but the time for chivalry had long gone. She went down in a heap at the foot of the stairs, the gown falling open once more. She was struggling to breathe and Louie momentarily thought he could have hit her too hard. She managed to rise into a crouch but was still hurting. Louie took a last look down at the beauty at his feet then crashed the gun down onto the back of her skull. This time she not so much fell as crumpled alarmingly back onto the carpet. The breasts were revealed in all their wonder and the taut body teased Louie to stay just a little longer. Somehow, he dragged his eyes away and made for the study. He wasn't interested now. It was a shame; under different circumstances....

Louie was in a hurry now. He had no idea how long he had been in the house but every instinct told him too long. Trouble was, so far he had little to show for his night's activities and he'd be damned if he was going to leave empty handed. He had no time to be fussy. He quickly scanned the study, broke open the desk, grabbed what came to hand and left quickly. He was almost back on the patio when he remembered the jewellery box on the landing. That would be it. Although there had been no shots, Louie was far from home turf and he'd had more than enough for one night. Christ, he had to be at work in less than four hours!

The pain in her head was blinding. Somebody was trying to carry her and she was in no state to argue. With every movement she struggled with nausea and the blinding lights in front of her eyes. She allowed herself to be carried and then felt a cold dampness on her forehead which brought its own wave of nausea which threatened to overwhelm her once more. Slowly she opened her eyes. Her sight swam into focus to alight on the misshapen face of Steve sitting over her. If she looked half as bad as he did then she must look dreadful. Steve's face was a mask of dried blood. Both eyes were nothing more than blackened squints either side of a badly broken nose which was still oozing blood. Steve dabbed at it absentmindedly with a blood stained cloth. She had no idea where his blood ended and hers began. Her attempts to get up were met with renewed waves of pain and nausea and Steve's anguished concern which came out as a frothing gargle and little more. He was sweet but the jewellery box had done little to improve his looks. (why do you think she had needed the coke ?) As the rest of the room came in to dull focus Terry was appalled at the amount of blood everywhere. The carpets were stained and trails lead from the bedroom to the stairs and back again ,where heavy footprints had trampled the blood deep into the pile. They were not alone.

'Perhaps we could have a few words, ma'am ?'

Questions, did she look like she needed questions now ?

The haul had not been worth it . The pieces were nice but he had little hope of getting anywhere close to market value for them . The desk had yielded nothing more than a bunch of papers which Louie had had little chance to look at. He was more concerned now with his own appearance. He surveyed his face now in the bathroom mirror, in what passed for his bathroom. It wasn't too bad. He had fallen heavily when he had been tripped but aside from that he looked pretty normal and he had secured a useful bonus. Guns had never been his scene but one thing was for sure, the Magnum could give him a nice edge.

The Pipeline 4)

In front of her stood what she assumed to be the closest thing the

cops could find to a detective but to her he just looked like an

overgrown college kid hopelessly trying to convince his peers that

he knew what he was doing. Nobody was buying it. Like every

other male in the room he was desperate to avoid looking at her

directly, he talked towards the corner of the room and only looked

at her fleetingly and even then her obvious femininity caused

colour to rise in his cheeks and spread across his face. Somehow

Terry didn't hold out much hope for anything that had been stolen

in this neck of the woods. Get it back, I don't think so.

Terry went through her story mechanically, it was easier to stick

close to the truth. Boy meets girl, boy beds girl, boy disturbs theft

in progress, boy and girl get hit - hard. She had had little chance to

do a complete inventory of the house. She knew her baubles were

gone. Seeing them on the floor was about the last thing she

remembered before the guys with the drills had moved into her head .Unfortunately they were still there and now they had very large boots on.

She managed to come up with a description but she already knew it could fit half the population of downtown Washington but it had at least got the cops off her back. No doubt they would be back.

Monday morning for Steve Gaynor was never a pleasant experience and having a close encounter with a jewel box had done nothing to improve his spirits. Although he was still playing the dissatisfied victim for the benefit of his work colleagues it had taken Steve all of two minutes to realise that the real loss was not one or two of Terry's trinkets (they could be replaced easily enough) but his briefcase. Admittedly the papers which had been inside were not exactly written in plain English but in the wrong hands it was pretty clear that the deal into the UK was delivering far more than a few hundred autos. The bank account details would seem a little bizarre, even for a relatively well-heeled motor executive but the regular deposits from England would be harder to square away. He tried to look on the bright side, chances are that your common or garden hood would simply throw the papers away, sell the briefcase and get rid of the jewellery. Sure, he would , happened everyday. Somehow, Steve couldn't even make himself believe it. What chance had he of convincing a federal jury. (Jesus ! Come on will you, this doesn't mean anything.)

Steve pushed his chair away from his desk and walked towards the coffee machine. It was no more than a simple b&e, so some papers had gone missing, so what. The cops didn't know anything about them. The bank accounts were in a different name and there was little to tie him in . Hell, tie him into what ? Even if the accounts were traced back to him (how the hell could they do that anyway ?) it wasn't illegal to have accounts in foreign countries. So he might have a little trouble with the IRS, big deal.

The phone burst into life and shattered Steve's comfortable illusion. The voice was new to him but it was the words which held his attention.

"I know who you are. I know what you're doing. I know where you live."

The phone went dead. Steve collapsed into his chair. It would all be much easier if his heart would just give up the unequal struggle right there. No nasty questions. No cops, no DEA. Would it be so bad ?

Unfortunately for Steve his heart continued to pound in his chest and slowly his other senses started to come back on line. So, somebody knew, how much would it take ? Jeez, he had a fortune in Switzerland. He had more money than most people could imagine. Even a couple of hundred grand would be manageable. The scam would still be in place. The way the market was at the moment he would make it back in a couple of months. He could handle this. No problem

----

'Would my right honourable friend care to comment on the latest

employment figures ?'

'I thank the right honourable gentleman and I am pleased to

announce that for the fourth quarter Her Majesty's government

has returned a drop in unemployment, four per cent latterly, which

contrasts somewhat radically with the woeful record of the

previous administration.

Once more our record continues to put to the lie the decline of our

manufacturing base and I can report with some glee that the

reports of the death of our manufacturing base have been

somewhat over exaggerated. I can only thank my right honourable

colleagues for their tireless work in their constituencies and

throughout the country which has played an integral part in

achieving this laudable situation'

Simon Parkinson sat down to a chorus of throaty support from the assembled back benchers who knew only too well what a radical turnaround had been achieved. In a few short months Simon Parkinson had blown into the DTi with all the reforming zeal of a Tv evangelist and his results had been no less startling. British industry had taken up its bed and walked. To be truthful it wasn't so much walking as running at record breaking pace towards a new dawn which had seen the UK become the focal point of relocating industries looking for a bolt-hole into the new Europe. But this was not just another false dawn based on short term political expediency. From the outset Simon Parkinson had set out an agenda which required industry to justify all political support backed by real plans, and more importantly measurable objectives. No longer was industry seen as the guru of change. Parkinson had realised that industry was just as much at fault as the rest of the system. In truth it had no more idea of where it was than education or health and only by demanding real measurement and strictly controlling investment to those areas where UK Ltd had a real chance to compete had he been able to save millions ploughed into short term businesses that would never pay in the long term and concentrate his resources into key areas where 'Made In Britain' really meant something and more importantly where the brands developed were not trying to compete on price but where success had been built on prestige products in strong sectors backed by real customer information. Sure ,you could buy the Japanese alternative, Korean products were always going to be cheaper and nobody built quality in better than the Yanks. But , for the first time Simon Parkinson had established 'Made In Britain' as the prestige centre of European manufacturing with brands that were being constantly developed not according to personal whim of the Directors but through radical thinking based on customer insight and up to the minute IT.

Naturally, there were detractors, this was Britain after all. In the last six months he had seen, heard or fielded everything from under age sex accusations to departmental fraud and family pressures. His position had not been helped by a further addition to his agenda which had, for the first time put government projects on a semi serious footing. The days of 'money for old rope' were coming to an end and a lot of high profile people were going to lose a great deal of UK and EEC funded gravy. Government projects now had real, achievable and measurable objectives. Funding was no longer based on how many 'bums' you had on seats (real or imaginary). Training had to show tangible benefits. If back to work programmes didn't get people back to work they were pulled. Giving the long term unemployed the opportunity to study for an MSc which was never going to help their employment prospects had been outlawed and more importantly, enforced within a few weeks of coming to power.

All this had been underscored with a real belief not in the established industries and their powerful lobbies which tied up new technology and innovation until they viewed it to be necessary but a belief instead in the new industries based on long term benefits to society as a whole rather than short term financial benefits for the minority. It sounded crass even now but Simon Parkinson had lived every word and had presided over what had amounted to a political economic revolution which had seen the UK become the centre for alternative transport technologies. Indeed, such was the scale of development that traditional car-based transport was now in the minority, not because of punitive taxation but because rapid transit and community services had been developed based on what people actually wanted rather than what the car lobby would allow.

Outwardly, this had all been achieved by a combination of political expediency, economic necessity and good old fashioned negotiation. In truth Simon Parkinson had an organisation that made Donnegan's North Eastern connections look like a junior school outing.

Sean felt like shit. Harry didn't see the need for blasphemy but that was Harry to a tee. Sean felt like shit and there was no getting away from it. He stared into his coffee and looked across at Harry. To be fair, Harry didn't look so good either. All the time Sean had been 'playing' at the 'plant' Harry had been left to take all the heat and try and figure out what it all meant.

"What I don't understand is how come a simple everyday homicide is generating so much shit? I mean, Jesus ! Everybody south of the Pope wants us to lay off and I expect his letter is somewhere in the goddamn post. I mean what gives ? "

The question drifted into focus in Sean's mind. Why was everybody

so goddamn keen to file this one in the bin? It was a good point. Be

damned if he could work it out now though. Sean looked up at

Harry's chart. All he could see was a bunch of bastards working to

keep them from finding Nicky Jenkins' killer and a whole bunch of

question marks. What had they really got ? Outwardly, Masters, the

suit from the plant was sweetness and light but wanted them out

just as soon as humanly possible. He had given nothing away and

with the August sales peak just a month or two away his need for a

quiet life had never been more important to him. 'Cherokees' with

optional drug overdose was something he could do without. Sean's

masterstroke of going undercover at the 'plant' had been about as

inconspicuous as your average bomb attack and he had learnt the

thin end of sod all. All he knew now was that he wasn't cut out to

be an 'associate'. Michaels had done his part by playing along but

any contact with anybody who had had contact with Mr. Jenkins

was just not going to happen. Harry's donkey work had come up with all sorts of unsavoury practises that appeared to be de rigeur

for any self respecting production plant but nothing to tie anybody

to Nicky Jenkins. Drugs, alcohol, petty theft, pornography, even

small time prostitution were all seen as lucrative side lines which,

so long as they didn't compromise the great God volume, were

tolerated, if not actively encouraged by the powers that be. Sean

was sure of one thing ,the Japs didn't do it like this.

After nine weeks of nothing Sean could pull out of his undercover

assignment without any more grief and Sean doubted whether

anyone would miss him. But where did they go from here ?

Sean looked across at Harry and noticed for the first time that Harry

was not a young man. Sean had always despised Harry 's mediocrity

but he also knew that Harry had the guts to do all the things that

Sean had never been able to face. Family, with all its responsibilities

was not something Sean had ever got around to and now guessed

he never would. Maybe they should dump the case for Harry's sake.

What did he have left , two years, three ? Sean was sorry to say he had no idea how old Harry was, but he sure looked like an old man now.

Under the chart was a mass of unanswered paperwork covering everything from car requisitions to fast food wrappers. Somewhere underneath it all Sean hoped he still had a desk.. For no real reason, Sean started to try and clear some of the debris. The top layer was just the beginning. Harry, normally so meticulous must have been under serious pressure to let it get this bad. A handwritten note caught Sean's attention, not least because it was written in an unintelligible script Sean didn't recognise as either his own drunken scrawl or Harry's sit-up-and beg style.

"What's this"

"I don't know , let me look"

Harry took the paper and stared at it as if seeking divine inspiration. Clearly, the Almighty was busy right now as Harry's brow remained in a dark furrow as he scoured his brain for some inkling of what this scrap was supposed to relate to. Suddenly, it came to him.

Harry breathed out slowly, thankful that his grey matter could still deliver even if it took a little longer than he would have liked.

"Copy of a B&E report from the house of one of the commercial managers at the plant. Some evidence of coke, but nothing heavy. Means nothing. Stands to reason, nine thousand people, got to be a crime of some sort everyday."

Harry looked away and continued musing over the wall chart. Sean continued to stare at the paper. Harry was right, probably meant nothing. Nothing really taken. Some jewellery, insurance would cover that. Description could fit half the cops in the room right now. The only interest seemed to come from the main witness. Sean tried to picture 'Terry'. Six foot of female caucasian who apparently knew just enough about guns to get herself into real trouble.

"Do you mind if I check it out ?. If I'm coming out of the plant I'll need something to get me back in the swing of things round here"

"Help yourself , there's more than enough for everyone" .

Harry swept his arm across the desk in an exaggerated gesture of generosity. Christ, there was enough paperwork to keep half the department going until next Thanksgiving.

Donnegan had always known that Steve Gaynor would be a liability. Of course he had known about the robbery before the cops had but he was not keen on the loss of the briefcase. Donnegan knew that Gaynor had no idea of the scale of the operation but he wondered about the missing papers. Jeez, what was the point of having Terry on site if Gaynor was going to do his own thing ? He could pull her out but with the cops sniffing around it would only look dodgy. Besides anybody who could fool Gaynor into believing there was some sort of commitment between them wouldn't have any trouble convincing a few cops of her innocence. It could still be contained. Gaynor would have an accident in a few months once the heat was off . Donnegan would have one of his people promoted. It would still work.

Donnegan rose from the desk at a discrete knock from the door and walked towards the corner of the room as the door opened and Terry announced her presence in the room. Donnegan was courteous as he showed her to a chair but his mood changed abruptly as he dealt a savage blow to her neck as she passed him on her way down to the chair. She fell awkwardly and caught the edge of the chair as she went down. Donnegan pushed the chair aside and struck her a second time this time full in the stomach leaving her doubled over with pain and gasping for breath. Coming on top of the brief but savage beating she had received at the hands of Louie Donnegan's blows were just reopening wounds which had just began to heal and which now announced their reappearance with stabbing pain crashing through her stomach and bright, bright lights spinning before her eyes. Donnegan helped her in to the chair as she broke down into soft quiet sobs which she tried her best to stifle. If she knew anything about Donnegan it was that he did not tolerate weakness and failure was simply not in his vocabulary. The breadth of his vocabulary was something that had never troubled

Donnegan and he dropped into his best gutter speak to address the

girl who was now far from the beauty Sean would have recognised.

"What the hell is the point of fucking Gaynor if you can't protect my

investment ?"

W ith these words Donnegan grabbed the back of the chair and

spun it round so that he could stare directly in to the once -

beautiful face. Terry lost her balance and sprawled helplessly back

towards the carpet. Donnegan's boot crashed into her side as he

repeated each word.

"What - the - fuck - is - the - point ?"

Terry had seen this before. She was not there to answer the

questions, just to take a beating and to recognise that Donnegan

controlled her every move. Who she slept with, when she slept with

them and how much it cost her.

Louie had finally got some time to check out his haul from the condo. The glass had been nice and would keep him in reasonable style for some time but it was the contents of the briefcase which held most interest. The case was full of bank statements dating back nearly six months from a bank in Switzerland that was receiving regular payments from the U.K. In truth he had no idea what Steve Gaynor was doing. He had no idea where the cash was coming from. What he did know was that there was a helluva lot of it and from his experience that amount of cash could only come from something illegal. He would squeeze Gaynor a little and see if he couldn't boost his modest haul with a little judicious blackmail. Gaynor would probably pay a few grand to keep the IRS off his back. Jesus, anybody would pay to keep the IRS off their backs.

Harry's home life was not quite as idyllic as Sean had imagined. Harry was never quite sure why they had never really socialised together, all he knew was that after a certain point it was a lot easier to leave work as work and draw a neat line underneath.

Harry knew that Sean was about as different from him as it was

possible for two human beings to be. But still their partnership had

endured over nearly six years of some of the hardest police work

Harry had ever known. Before Sean ? What had life been like before

Sean ? Before Sean Harry had had a succession of partners fresh

out of college eager to learn the ropes and move on to whatever

they believed was better than this. Harry knew that it didn't get a

helluva lot better than this. He was pretty much left to run his own

investigations (only this latest case was different) . So long as he got

results he was left alone and that was the way he had liked it until

Sean had shown up. Despite all their differences they worked well

together although neither would admit as much. Harry had only

heard rumours of Sean's past. He had been married, he knew that

and he sure didn't have too many fans in the department. He could

only guess at what Sean's life was like outside of the office. There

had been a number of women but none seemed to stay too long .

There was the usual retreat behind drink but Sean had always come out the other side. Sometimes stronger, sometimes just quieter. Nothing could contrast more with his own life outside of the job. Even now, he could hardly hazard a guess at what Sean was doing whilst Harry sat crouched over a beer staring intently into the middle distance. One of the reasons Harry guessed he and Sean never really met outside of the office was that Harry never really left the office. Harry relaxed by working. In his den he had all the usual kit but alongside one wall Harry had a complete duplicate of his desk at the office. (only without most of the crap - thankfully, Jean had always seen to that) The same desk, the same pinboard and right now, the same dead ends.

Harry stared at the players. Nicky Jenkins - Michaels - Masters - Sean - himself . Steve Gaynor - Terry Collins. Harry had no idea whether they were involved or not. Their names were placed in a separate section of the board, they were connected to the 'plant' and Harry was loathe to take them off as then they had precious little to show for nearly ten weeks work. Underneath Harry knew

that if he had pinned up everything that Sean had seen or heard

about in the plant he'd need a bigger house. Nicky Jenkins was still

dead. All the pins in Christendom couldn't change that.

Harry had done everything Sean hadn't. He had married young and

never looked back. Jean had always been there for him. Theirs was

not exactly a demonstrative relationship but she had seen him

through more shit than he cared to remember. Together they'd put

two boys through college and carved out a decent niche in not-so-

decent-neighbourhood. Harry knew he wasn't destined for great

things. Jean knew Harry wasn't destined for great things but naked

ambition had been replaced by the secure backing of a good man

who had never put a foot wrong in over thirty years of marriage.

Jean had never liked Sean and Harry had kept them apart and

hostilities had been avoided.

Harry stared at the board and decoded that Steve Gaynor would

warrant further investigation. All, their other leads sure as hell weren't going anywhere and if Steve could check out the robbery

than he would look at the background of Mr. Gaynor.

What Sean was actually doing would not have brought a smile to

Harry's face. Whilst not exactly inviting a visit from Internal Affairs

Sean was about to bring himself into play in a game he didn't

understand with stakes he could ill afford. He stood now outside

Steve Gaynor's condo feeling like a nervous date on prom night. He

knocked casually and stood back from the door. A light came on

over the porch and Sean could hear bolts sliding back. Slowly the

door opened held by a chain and Terry peered out into the night.

Sean prided himself on his imagination but his picture hadn't even

come close. Terry was hardly your run of the mill female caucasian.

The problem was, she knew it and seemed to take some sort of

perverse pleasure in reducing DEA men to dumb-struck , gibbering

adolescents.

Sean tried manfully to marshal his senses and, if truth be told was

pretty impressed with what he achieved. Outwardly at least he was

the epitome of professionalism even if inside his hormones were

dancing gigs he thought had long since been forgotten.

"Do you mind if we get this over with. I've already told you guys

everything. How hard can this be ? Simple robbery goes wrong, I

lost a few necklaces - get out there and find the sonafabitch."

Sean had to admit it sounded pretty easy. OK, so Terry and

boyfriend did a little coke now and then. Christ, if the DEA arrested

everyone who did 'a little coke' the pens would be full by Thursday.

"yes, Miss........?"

"Collins, Terry Collins - look my name is in the report, my address is

in the report, my report is in the report. You could read it ye'know"

Sean had to admit she had got the attitude down pretty good and if

truth be told he was just looking for a reason to continue talking to

her , even if it was blindingly obvious.

"Just the gems you say, nothing else ?"

"No, Nothing else. We surprised him, he didn't leave a card, he's not on our Christmas card list."

Surprised him , was hardly the word. Terry doubted if any hood had ever looked more surprised. Being jumped by a gun toting semi - clad beauty can do that to a man.

"Perhaps you could check out some pictures Miss, it would help"

"Yeah, right"

The door closed and then re-opened as Sean was admitted into a hall which showed little evidence of its recent adventures. Sean guessed the carpet was new and he could smell new paint.

Sean was holding a stack of mug shots from the office . He should have done this downtown but he knew this was a better way. It was more private and it kept Terry away from the rest of the department. Sean wasn't sure why that was important, he just knew it was and if he had learnt anything over the last twenty years it was to trust his instincts.

His hormones were starting to kick in and Sean was inwardly

annoyed that Gaynor was around. Again, he had no idea what he

was getting into to but he just didn't need the ever present

gargoyle that had become Steve Gaynor looking over his shoulder,

guarding his woman from his questions. Aside from the remodelling

courtesy of the jewellery box, Steve Gaynor was now as insecure as

hell. Sean put this down to having the DEA on his doorstep but

Steve Gaynor was jumpy as hell and Sean found it difficult to settle

with him in the room. Perhaps going downtown would have been a

better idea. If truth be told Sean had been acting on auto pilot

ever since he had entered the house. His brain had taken over,

gone through the well practised clichés whilst his imagination had

gone into overdrive. Terry was siting beside him now slowly turning

the pages of the books scanning the faces of Washington's finest.

Sean was struggling to stay in control. He was convinced that

Gaynor could feel the tension in the apartment and it had very

little to do with the crime so recently committed there. Terry was wearing a cream top which buttoned low in the front and Sean was

acutely aware of the hint of cleavage that was all too apparent

when Terry leaned to turn to turn the pages. She had drawn her

legs up under her and the skirt was stretched across slim thighs.

Downtown would have been a much better idea.

The Pipeline: (5)

Harry had reached one conclusion. Steve Gaynor was not a nice

piece of work. Initially he had appeared innocuous enough. He had

gone through the usual academic hoops which had immediately

endeared him to Harry who had never had such privileges. His rise

through the ranks had been pretty unremarkable and what

progress there had been did not appear to have come from

personal ability. It was surely just a coincidence that his father was

European Sales Director. Steve Gaynor had studied Business Studies

at a minor University where his academic studies had been

interrupted by a series of minor legal infringements and brushes

with the local police. All had been smoothed over by judicious use

of his father's money.

There had been an unsuccessful marriage which had lasted barely a

few months and the unfortunate girl appeared to have disappeared from the face of the earth after some legal wrangling over a not insubstantial settlement. Steve Gaynor had installed himself in an uptown apartment where a succession of highly attractive and equally unsuitable women had crossed briefly into his life and left just as quickly. Before Terry Collins there had been nothing even remotely close to permanence for three years and then Gaynor had returned with the deal and the girl.

Unremarkably, he had followed his father into the car industry where he had climbed the promotional ladder at an unremarkable pace by doing nothing remarkable. He had become responsible for a number of minor markets where he could indulge his wanderlust at the company's expense without too much attention being drawn to his volume achievements. All this had changed with what appeared to be a significant coup on Steve's part following a trip to the North East of England , which although not initially his responsibility had resulted in a significant jump in his volumes and the opening of a new import and inspection facility in a market which was now on schedule to take close to a thousand units a year. How did someone with Gaynor's track record suddenly bring home the deal of the decade? Harry suspected that his father had had more than a guiding hand in the deal but there was nothing to say it wasn't all totally legit. The smell of nepotism rose out of Harry's investigation but as much as it sickened him there wasn't a law against it. Harry had added all this on to the chart but it still was nothing more than a lot of unrelated names and faces. So, promotion at the plant wasn't purely based on merit. (welcome to industry ! This was nothing new - the Police Department wasn't exactly holier than thou). So what ? Harry stared now at the chart and tried to find the elusive piece which he knew would link the whole sorry mess.

Jean stood at the door of the office and looked across to Harry where he pored over the desk. She had always been pleased with her choice. She took the coffee over to him and looked at the chart. The names meant nothing to her. She knew of 'the plant' of course but the actual people were just names. Harry had written the connections between the various groups of people and as she read so Jean became less and less impressed with the local industry and the sorry mess of nepotism, exploitation and petty crime that seemed to be the very essence of the place.

Sean already knew he was in deep water. Terry was beginning to mean far more to him than was strictly necessary for the investigation and way more than his emotions were in any fit state to handle. The way he had it figured, so long as Terry didn't get to realise he was probably safe. His life was still his own. (Jesus ! Yeah his life was still his own. He was free to eat endless pizza alone. Free to pursue his two equally destructive pastimes of heavy drinking and meaningless, soul less sex just as long as he wanted. He was free to pretend that everything was just dandy !) . Sean wasn't sure how much Terry had put together. Sure, she must have felt something between them when they wee at the apartment and she was smart enough to realise that Sean hadn't needed to take her to dinner and she hadn't needed to say yes. (Christ, for some kind of go-ahead guy you sure can second guess you're way out of something good!). Sean had used the pretence of official business once more but since then he had not mentioned work again and their conversation had ranged over myriad subjects from politics and finance to people and football. If Sean was honest with himself (now, that would be a first) he hated the thought of Terry and Steve together but he was hardly in a position to start laying down the law and Sean was scared to admit that he cared that much. Problem was he did and he knew it.

Simon Parkinson's official first line read like a 'Who's Who' of British industrial and commercial interests and it had been this willingness to involve benchmark companies and individuals with the presence to match that had marked out Parkinson's ministry from previous administrations. For the first time British policies were being forged by people who really knew what was going on and had the balls to

push change no matter how unpalatable it was to the vested

interests that had for years effectively run the show to the

detriment of the country and the people.

Change costs and the radical changes across the UK had been

funded by drugs cash on an unprecedented scale. Old industries

had been paid off, directors retired, new blood inducted into the

new way of thinking.

Simon Parkinson intended to be in power for quite some time to

come. The move into power had allowed an embryonic business

empire based firmly in the black economy to become the lynch pin

which was in the process of turning the fertile grounds of Western

Europe into the drug ravaged inner cities of downtown Washington.

Under the guise of legitimate business expansion Parkinson had

orchestrated the biggest growth in illegal drug trafficking and

thusfar it had all been accomplished cleanly and quietly.

Parkinson had borrowed from a number of disciplines. Each

industry believed it was acting in total isolation. Each team knew

only its own team members, each stage of each operation had no

visibility of the next tier above or below. Drugs had been flowing

freely into the UK through standard products in standard containers

for nearly eighteen months but it was the colonisation of Britain by

large scale manufacturing operations that was providing the real

volume. Trafficking had never been contemplated on this scale and

it was steadily making Simon Parkinson a very rich man indeed.

Simon Parkinson's unofficial first line however had an altogether

different brief. Donnegan had been a member of Parkinson's first

line since the inception of 'the pipeline' and if truth be told it took

just such a scheme or something similar to get Parkinson's

attention. (O.K. so Parkinson was taking a twenty five per cent cut

but the clout that that delivered meant it was worth every penny

and then some.) Donnegan had long admired Parkinson's style. On

the hustings he was a sight to behold and as a public speaker he had few betters. With his wide ranging reforms and his openness to new ideas he had marked a seed change in British politics and whilst at present he was content to remain as the power behind the throne few would have bet against a bid for the party leadership and a move to Downing Street. But Donnegan had seen Parkinson's alter ego in operation and it wasn't pretty . As his underground operation had grown inevitably there had been slip ups and having experienced Parkinson's wrath over the minor disruption to 'the pipeline' when Jenkins had stalled the system he was not keen to repeat the experience. He had seen Parkinson's wrath at close quarters and it was such a stark contrast to the public face that Donnegan had shivered involuntarily.

Every month Parkinson chaired a meeting of his unofficial first line when progress was closely monitored and links forged between elements of Parkinson's growing network. Donnegan couldn't remember what had sparked Parkinson's outburst but he had seen him drag George Weston , an industrialist from the South of

England, over his desk by his hair and hurl him against the oak panelling that lent his office an air of sophistication that in truth was far divorced from reality. Weston had then received a brutal beating while the rest of the group had stayed routed to their chairs shocked by the scene in front of them and yet powerless to intervene. It had served to instil a discipline in to the group that was close to a religious fervour. Whilst they were all becoming rich and powerful men in their own fiefdoms, here Parkinson was the boss and they would do well to remember that. Donnegan had made a mental note not to cross Parkinson, at least not whilst he was still in the country.

Thankfully, Donnegan had been able to report significant success even during the police investigation. The mention of the police had not been received well but the sheer volume of heroin that was flowing into England was enough to stifle any concerns and the fact that supply had remained unaffected spoke volumes for

Donnegan's organisation and he knew he was now held in some

esteem at least by his peers around the table.

Terry was sitting at a table with her back to the door. Sean had time

to appreciate the curve of her neck, the regal posture before

moving across and laying his arm across her shoulders. She looked

up and Sean knew he was in even more trouble than even he had

realised. He was in good company. Terry had been trying to

disentangle her feelings from her responsibilities and had got

nowhere. It wasn't supposed to be like this. She was not keen to

rediscover the darker side of Donnegan's character and yet things

were hardly going to plan. As far as Donnegan was concerned Terry

was still watching Steve Gaynor and yet here she was sitting down

with the officer charged with the investigation of Jenkins alleged

murder and actually enjoying it. She was out of control . She slept

with Steve because she was told to. She would sleep with Sean because she loved him. She did what she was told because she knew Donnegan would kill her.

The evening wasn't going well. Terry knew that Sean could sense her indecision and Sean was convinced that this latest foray into the emotional whirlpool which was his social life was about to go bottom up just like all the others. He could hardly blame her. Washed up were the words that sprang to mind. Sean rose to get up,

"What do you say to calling it a day now, you seem pretty distracted and I've got some work to do ? I'll drop you off but I need to go to the office first. "

Sean pushed his chair back. He had lied about the work but he could always go and check on Harry, God knows he had hardly been pulling his weight recently. Sean doubted if Harry would have gone home.

They drove in near silence until Sean pulled up outside the precinct house.

"Are you coming up, if you're lucky this'll be the only chance you get to see the inside of a DEA office."

Sean hated that about himself - he could always make a joke. His personal life was headed for the toilet (again) but he could still joke. Terry climbed out of Sean's battered Pontiac and followed Sean up the steps. She was still preoccupied but it would be good to see Harry again. Terry had taken a liking to Harry, not in the same way as she saw Sean but in a secure, fatherly way. Maybe he could see a way out of this mess.

Sean lead the way up two flights. The building was in darkness apart from the duty desk and a couple of lights burning deep in the heart of the structure. Their heels echoed on the floors and shadows played around the walls. Given Terry's relationship with Donnegan this was not somewhere she ever wanted to come without Sean. Ahead of her, Sean turned off the corridor and headed into one of the darker corners where a reading light was burning brightly on a desk and where Harry was staring intently at the wall. Maybe he couldn't help her after all. As they got closer Harry rose to meet

them and held out his hand to Sean . It was a little formal but Terry

was touched by the gesture. He was considerably less formal as she

reached him. He hugged her warmly and asked how she was doing.

Terry was not surprised Harry knew that Sean had been seeing her

and maybe he wanted it to work out. Officially, as part of an

ongoing investigation she shouldn't be in the office , but as a

witness to minor theft Harry was not about to start quoting the

book now. Terry looked up the chart and was shocked to see her

own name up there along with probably the worst photograph of

herself she had ever seen. Slowly she traced the various links

across the chart. A lot of them ended in question marks or pictures

of other people that Terry did not recognise. Except for one. Terry

looked intently at the chart and studied the face. Right now, she

was at a crossroads. She could say nothing and walk away or she

could put in a link that Harry knew nothing about. To do so would

mean that her links with Donnegan would almost certainly come out and everything she had with Sean would be put in jeopardy.

Slowly, she picked up some of Harry's string and a couple of pins.

She pushed the pins into place next to hers and another picture

which said Louie Jameson next to it and tied the string between the

pins. Harry looked bewildered.

"I don't get it, what connection have you got with Jameson ?

Terry looked across at Sean, took a deep breath and sat down;

" Louie Jameson is the guy who broke into the apartment. I didn't

know he worked at the plant , but its definitely him. I wouldn't

forget him in a hurry."

Harry and Sean had finally got a break. Unfortunately it was going

to help the robbery squad more than them but at least they had a

link to the plant which hadn't been there before. Maybe it would

also give them some leverage to get some real information about

what had really happened to Nicky Jenkins. God knows it was about

time they made some headway.

Sean looked like the last thing he wanted was to be reminded of

Steve Gaynor. Terry's relationship with Steve was something that

he had tried to wipe from his mind.

Harry, on the other hand looked positively elated and was already

planning to bring Louie back in for questioning and he could begin

to see that maybe all this work was actually going to get

somewhere.

Terry had a straight choice. By linking herself to Louie Jameson she

knew she had put herself in danger. If Louie found out that she had

identified him (and who else could ?) he would almost certainly try

something. He knew where she lived and the police couldn't hold

him forever. If Terry asked for protection from Donnegan she would

have to explain why she was talking to the police. If she said

nothing and Louie came back to the apartment then it would all be

over. If she asked Sean for help she would have to tell him how she

was involved and what that made her. (Life just didn't get any

better than this)

Terry sat down and took a deep swallow of Harry's coffee.

"All this is not what it seems. Sean, you have to know that before I say any more you must know that I love you and I never wanted to hurt you. I know you don't like Steve but we're only involved because I'm there to check up on him. I work for a guy named Donnegan. Steve does too, but Donnegan doesn't trust him so he had me move in and look after him. I'm sorry I never wanted you to find out this way."

Terry was in tears as she finished and turned away from Sean.

Harry held her and lead her to the stairs. He took her down to the car lot and put her in his car.

"Stay here, I'll not be long"

Harry walked back into the office. Sean was leaning on the desk. He looked as if his whole world had suddenly come to a sickening halt. He had not held anything close for such a very long time and now that he had dared to believe that there might be something good for him after all she was nothing more than a cheap hooker paid to sleep with some sleaze. (Christ - you sure can pick 'em) . Harry opened the desk drawer and took out two glasses. From the filing cabinet he took out a bottle of bourbon and poured two generous measures. Sean took it as tears welled up. The liquid burned his throat but it felt good. Too good.

Terry had blown it. She had gambled on Sean's feelings and he had been found wanting. From Harry's car she had seen him get in his car and drive away. She hadn't seen him since. Harry had moved her into his house. Jean hadn't said a word as if Harry was regularly in the habit of taking in waifs and strays. Terry knew Donnegan would know what was happening and it was only a matter of time before Louie was helping the police with their enquiries. Louie would go to jail, Harry would want his home back and she would get the beating of her life from Donnegan. Wasn't life sweet.

The Pipeline: (6)

Louie wasn't smiling anymore. Having a witness changed

everything. They could place him in the house, at the time and they

could put him away any time they wanted. He had got rid of most

of the stones but he still had Gaynor's briefcase. He hadn't really

had a chance to put the frighteners on Gaynor but maybe it would

be enough to give him something to negotiate with.

Louie was singing like a canary and Harry's chart just wasn't big

enough to chart the implications and connections. What had

started out as a straight forward robbery was now a full-scale

investigation linking the robbery at Gaynor's apartment, the minor

drug circles at the plant and more importantly the export orders

that Steve Gaynor had been instrumental in making happen. Terry

had known nothing of the deal that was taking Cherokees with added options into Europe, Harry was convinced of that, but quite

how he was going to bring it all down he had no idea. This was

Sean's party or at least it would have been but Sean had taken

early retirement with Jim Beam and Harry didn't see him coming

back anytime soon. .

Louie had used the contents of Steve's briefcase to make a deal and

the sheer scale of what appeared to be happening was starting to

scare the hell out of Harry. Now all the pressure to drop the case

started to make sense. The $64,000 question was where did Harry

go with this ? Louie knew nothing more than the briefcase had

given up. Steve Gaynor was more hurt by Terry's defection than he

was by the prospect of serious charges but to be honest Harry

wasn't exactly sure what he was guilty of. Sure, he was an accessory

to a major drug smuggling operation but he couldn't name

anybody. He knew nothing about the details of the deal and would

only serve to alert the real power that the DEA knew what was

going on. Pulling Steve in made no sense at all. Harry had managed to put most of the new information on to the chart and with Jean

they had established that Cherokees had been leaving the States

for the UK for the last eighteen months each one holding

approximately 2 kilos of heroin. . Over the same period General

Motors had shipped 1700 units to the UK which equalled one

helluva lot of drugs.

What Harry needed was some high level clout. He couldn't trust

anybody in the department and he had no idea how far up the

money had reached. He could really do with someone from outside

with enough power to push through whatever charges were

necessary and with enough conviction to close down the operation

at each successive level just as the one above it became known.

Harry didn't have that sort of power. To make any of this happen

Harry was going to need some support from the UK and here he

was operating completely in the dark. He doubted if a brief

stopover in London counted as local knowledge. He had considered

bringing in the FBI but if the dirt had reached that high then he would soon be joining Mr. Jenkins and meeting a very nasty end indeed. Harry had avoided drugs for the last forty five years and he was too old to take his first trip now.

Harry was sure for the time being he was safe. Louie would not be missed yet and he was not an integral part of the operation so Harry believed that the alarm would not be raised yet. Steve Gaynor had not been arrested and Harry knew this was risky. He was betting that Gaynor had told no-one about losing the briefcase so here again so long as Gaynor kept his mouth shut (and who did he know to tell ?) Harry had some time.

Harry and Jean had considered the scene from every possible angle but it had taken Sean's reappearance to pull the beginnings of a plan together. Sean had simply walked back into the office and they had picked up where they had left off. True he looked like he hadn't slept for several days and he had visibly aged. His eyes were blood shot and sunken into his skull but Harry knew better than to draw attention to it. Sean appeared to have forgotten that Terry had ever existed and Harry knew better than to remind him He was just glad that Sean was back.

Together they had determined that what they needed was a foolproof plan where they could expose the full glory of the operation without putting themselves in any danger. Harry was thankful that Terry had already been moved out of town. Harry and Jean would leave immediately for the country. All locations were kept secret even between the three of them, with only phone booths and times for contacts. The captain wouldn't even have that. Only when the media started to report good news would they resurface. Sean would break the story and then they would see what exploded out of the woodwork. He would go to Congress and ask for support nationally and from the UK.

. The captain would have to co-ordinate it from here on in. He wouldn't be working out of the office. In short, Harry and Sean had done all they could to protect themselves and their loved ones. The only difference being that for Sean the list of loved ones was very

short indeed.

Sean only knew his congressman by sight. They had never met but

he was pretty sure that 'the pipeline' had not reached this far. Even

if it had Harry was safe and Sean had precious little to live for

anyway. Sean sat now outside a nondescript office in a nondescript

government building. Grey appeared to be the order of the day .

Sean really didn't care. (could have been Masters' office - how long

ago had that been ?) .Across the room a secretary, who, under

different circumstances Sean could have found attractive, was

typing into a word processor. She rose now as the office door

opened and she ushered him into a large oak panelled office that

was clearly designed to make its occupants feel very secure and

blessed by the goodness of the USA. The effect was totally wasted

on Sean. He walked over to the desk where a silver haired man was

rising from the desk to meet him.

"Take a seat son, you look like you need it "

Sean had never taken kindly to being addressed as 'son' and now was not a good time to see if his preference had changed.

Nevertheless, he sat down and tried to relax. The silver haired man introduced himself,

"William Boyd II, what can I do for you son?

Sean let it go a second time and shook William Boyd's hand,

"Call me Billy, everyone does. I hope you don't mind but I have taken the liberty of inviting in a friend of mine from across the pond. Sean Mason, may I introduce the right honourable Simon Parkinson. Mr Parkinson is the minister responsible for Trade & Industry in the UK. I hope you don't mind. "

"No, not at all, what we need is some heavy duty support. If Mr Parkinson can make that happen so much the better."

"Please call me Simon. I've never been a fan of titles. I'd rather we talked as colleagues."

Sean was not at ease and Simon Parkinson was not a colleague. Still if he could close it all down and put the culprits away then he would at least give the man the time of day.

For the next two hours Sean translated Harry's chart into words of one syllable for the Congressman and into English for Simon Parkinson. As he laid out the skeleton of the 'pipeline' Simon Parkinson became ever more intent and Sean realised that behind the political bonhomie was a very sharp cookie indeed. The Congressman (Sean had already forgotten his name) was clearly out of his depth and simply looking to push the whole thing further up the pole without soiling his hands. Maybe Parkinson would be enough. There were still gaps, Harry , Jean and Sean had put a lot of it together, all they wanted to do now was to see a major swoop by the guys in the white hats to close it all down. Sean had kept their names out of it . He knew Harry was traceable but he had all but wiped Terry from his mind so creating an informer was easy enough and had been an act of self preservation as much as anything. Sean was good at self preservation. He needed to be.

Just before six Sean finally stopped and took a long breath. Parkinson had filled several pads with copious notes whilst the Congressman looked shell-shocked. Sean felt elation and exhaustion in equal parts and just wanted to sleep and forget he had ever heard of goddamn Gaynor and the pain that he had brought. Sean had no idea what he was going to do now. He walked down the steps outside the courthouse and stepped wearily into his Camaro. Parkinson had wanted to take him into protective custody straight away but Sean had reasoned that at the moment only one person knew where he was going and he'd rather it stayed that way. He would only commit to further phone calls and both Parkinson and the Congressman (what the hell was his name ?) had both passed over secure phone numbers although the look on the Congressman's face was more akin to blind panic rather than reforming zeal and Sean was already wishing he hadn't bothered.

So long as it was only ignorance Sean could probably live with it.

Anything else could be dangerous.

Sean drove slowly for six blocks checking his baffles every now and

again and only when he was convinced he hadn't been followed did

he nurse the ageing Camaro beyond the legal limit and out of the

city. Right now Montana looked like a pretty good place to be. Sean

drove steadily for four hours. He stopped only once to check in with

Harry and to let him know how the meeting had gone. Sometime

before eleven Sean pulled into a motel and checked in. For the first

time in a very long time Sean slept for the best part of twelve hours.

In his mind Sean saw the powers of justice moving into position and

the triumph of the vanquished. In truth, something very different

was getting under way.

This was getting messy and Simon Parkinson did not like mess. .

Parkinson could live with the removal of minor irritations like

Jenkins but taking out Congressmen was not something he cared to sully his hands with. This was Donnegan's problem and by God Donnegan was going to clear it up. Mr. Mason was going to be no pushover and taking him out alone would only draw attention and send his partners in law and order scurrying into deeper holes. Mason had refused point blank to name names but it wouldn't be hard to find out who he had been assigned to and whether he had any personal connections that could be used against him. Somewhere , somebody would provide the leverage he needed , then it was just a matter of time. Now Parkinson needed to keep some distance between himself and Donnegan - the further the better. He'd be damned if a minor irritation in Washington was going to put the whole network in danger. If Donnegan nipped Mason in the bud then nothing would be lost except a congressman past his sell-by date and a couple of no-name cops. If Donnegan went down then Parkinson needed to limit the damage and then get a new 'pipeline' started as quickly as possible. All of which was

manageable.

Donnegan wasn't having a good day. Terry had gone absent without

leave, Gaynor was nowhere to be found and he was starting to get

a very bad feeling indeed. Outwardly, nothing had changed. The

'pipeline' was operating faultlessly but Donnegan was uneasy

without Terry. He was supposed to decide when she got pulled out

- declaring UDI was not something he had considered. However, all

of this was about to go into considerably sharper focus. At his

elbow the phone buzzed and Donnegan reached for it

automatically. The bizarrely distorted voice of The Right

Honourable Simon Parkinson bellowed across his desk as the

scrambler manipulated the sounds into a grotesque robotic

disembodied voice which he had only ever heard in his nightmares.

Donnegan listened stunned as Parkinson laid open the shattered

remains of his organisation and made it very clear what would happen if the network was put in jeopardy. The finer nuances were lost in the trickery of the electronics but the point was clear.

Donnegan was on trial.

His options were clear. Find Terry. Kill Boyd. Kill Mason. Do it now and do it fast.

Unknown to Sean, Harry and Jean had headed towards the coast, travelling down the eastern seaboard until they got to Annapolis where they mingled with the tourists, got some sun and waited for the fallout. Harry had called in some favours and taken a boat on the harbour. He could see anything coming a long way off and there were worse ways of killing time. If he was honest he could take any amount of this and he had just begun to believe that he had started his retirement five years early and it was all behind him now. It was years since he and Jean had spent any serious time away with each other and if anything they were closer now than at any time throughout their thirty years together.

Harry would never have seen it. Harry knew even less about

Congress than Sean so the passing of just another public servant

hardly registered with him. For Harry it was just another day in

hiding. He would have missed it, but Jean didn't and it brought

reality crashing home .Congressman William Boyd II had been

found in the early hours of yesterday morning at home and it

appeared he had died peacefully in his sleep. There were the usual

eulogies from the great and the good but nothing could disguise the

fact that two weeks ago Sean had been talking to William Boyd II

("call me Billy, everyone does") and now he was dead. Had he

started things moving or did Harry and Sean have to start over ?

Over the last two weeks Sean and Harry hadn't spoken but now

Harry needed reassurance that it was just unlucky and anytime

soon the media would be full of rather more pleasant news.

Jesus - what a mess . Terry didn't know much but she knew mess

and this was a doozy. In the last four days she had had plenty of time to reflect on the last three months and even to her it read like a very bad 'B' movie script. All she needed was some special effects and a monster made out of styrofoam and the effect would be complete. The only real difference was that real people were dead. Three months ago she had been a penniless nobody wandering aimlessly in the sun and not really caring where she went or how she paid for it. Initially Donnegan had been fun. He had looked after her like few men she had ever known with no question of payback ever arising and she had enjoyed the attention and played it to its full . She had assumed that working for Donnegan would involve little more than formalising her duties and having her own cash. Even Gaynor had seemed like a good idea at the time, although she'd be damned if she could remember now how it had seemed so appealing. Since then , she had been involved in a robbery, slept with Steve for money (she couldn't yet bring herself to call it whoring), continued to report back Steve's every move to Donnegan until she had turned her back on him in favour of Sean.

Great move . Poor Sean. If only he'd known what a nightmare she

would bring. Now she was damned. Like Harry and Jean she had

headed out of town to wait for things to blow over and for the guys

in the white hats to clear up the mess. She guessed Donnegan

would be looking for her but she had been a shiftless wanderer

before he met her and she could be again. Sean wasn't that

important, was he ?

Whilst Sean was heading to the wide open spaces of Montana and

Harry had headed down the coast to Annapaolis Terry had headed

north across the border into Canada. She had no connections there

and Toronto was as good as anywhere to get lost. She could do

without Donnegan and Sean would find someone else.

Her Mum would be impressed. Ten 'O' levels , four 'A' levels three

years at college and so far all she had to show for it were a string of

worthless relationships, the clothes she stood up in and a resume

with whore as her last occupation. Her Mum would be real

impressed.

Terry had a gift, that much she knew already. A gift for picking the wrong guy at the right time, or the right guy at the wrong time or some combination that was never what God had intended. On the few occasions she had got even remotely close to finding anything close to the right guy at the right time her self destruct sequence had kicked in and she had either created so much drama the poor 'schmo' in question had hit the nearest exit or she had decided in some bizarre corner of her brain that he would leave so better to get out first before she had to handle the hurt his way. It was a nice, secure way of making sure that she never got what she wanted. Sean was just the latest. He sure as shit wasn't the first and she doubted he would be the last. I guess you could say she had it sussed. Tomorrow would be the first day of the rest of her life.

Tomorrow wasn't the first day of the rest of her life. It was just like yesterday had been . She was still knackered, penniless and alone - wasn't life grand. The only real difference was that now she had decided to get her act together. It shouldn't be too hard to get a job

, at least her looks could get her that far and the rest would just

follow .

The Pipeline: (7)

The phone call from Harry had not come at a good time. For the

first time in a very long time Sean had taken the chance to take a

long hard look at his life and it wasn't pretty. A failed marriage, a

habitual drinking problem and precious little to show for more than

twenty years of upholding good - Protecting and Serving. A long

succession of superficial, short term attachments which had never

come close to breaching his defences culminating in his latest

emotional fuck up, Terry. If there was a scout badge for 'emotional

basket case' Sean reckoned he would qualify easily. Christ, he wrote

the book.

His had actually started out as quite a reasonable life. He had none

of the normal excuses. Stable home, both parents, older sister, no

crime. (so why had it all turned to shit ?) The Police Academy had

seemed a like a good idea, Wisconsin was hardly the drugs capital

of the world and yet he had gone out of his way to court trouble.

From some views his life was positively peachy and yet he had

contrived to take all that was good and turn it bad. (What a gift).

Fay had been way beyond him, it was a nice safe way to play the

mating game without the remotest possibility that he would have

to let anybody in or find anybody who would want to come in . It

was a perfect personal sabotage plan , guaranteed to make sure

that he would never have that which he craved most. But she had

consented to a night out with the fledgling beat bobby and she had

given him a chance to show off his dress uniform like it meant

something. Sean smirked as he thought about it now. She had

shocked with the pictures she had conjured up involving his

handcuffs and she had been as good as her word. He had seen a

side of her that only he knew about and they had laughed like

school kids through the whole thing. Even then, he was secretly

waiting for the illusion to end and in the end it was his own

insecurities which had fucked it up. Not another man, not another

woman just Sean becoming more and more paranoid that such a

great woman couldn't possibly want to stay with him. So she didn't.

The trust which had always been unspoken was questioned,

schedules scrutinised and suspects questioned. In truth, Sean had

spent more energy on undermining his marriage than he had ever

put into a case - he was that insecure. Or he had been. He had

driven Fay away . Hell, he had done more than that. He had bought

her the car, paid for the lessons and handed her the keys. He would

give anything to have her back.

The house had gone, and most of the friends had sided with Fay

and who could blame them ? The move to the DEA had been borne

out of a desperate need to move on, and the realisation that

promotions were always going to go to somebody else all the time

he stayed where he was. Harry had welcomed him into the

department and, if truth be told they had formed a good team.

There had been occasional lapses but they had worked well

together despite what Sean saw as huge differences between them.

Sean sat back , took a long drag on the cigar and sipped smoothly

from his glass - Perrier - for Chissakes - Yeah right, huge differences

! The only real difference was that Harry had everything Sean could

have had and Sean envied him so bad it hurt.

Sean leaned back and took a long swig from the bottle . The liquid

was positively anaemic. What he wouldn't give for the rasp of a real

drink. He had no idea what he would do now. The plan had only

gone as far as getting all four of them out of the senate in one

piece. There had been no contingencies for reunions, pleasant or

otherwise. Harry's call whilst unscheduled was not altogether

unsurprising - they were mates after all. Harry's tone however,

immediately put Sean on edge - this wasn't a 'how about goin' to

the ballgame' type of call. Sean listened intently as Harry laid out

what he and Jean had managed to glean form the papers since their

curiosity had been piqued by the death of the senator. In truth, the

death of William Boyd II has hardly caused a great stir across the

nation. Hell, it had hardly caused a stir in his own state. He had not been a young man. His political works had been enough to keep him comfortably off in the eyes of the electorate but they were never going to take him to the White House and whilst the 'loss of a great natural statesman' had brought all the usual plaudits from the great and the good, in truth the jockeying to be his successor had already begun and nobody seemed to care.

Harry laid out what they knew and Sean listened but what it really came down was simple. Had anything been done? Sean had never held out much hope for 'Billy' Boyd, he had far more faith in the Englishman , Parkinson; but he still needed to know whether he had to start all over again and if he had to, how much more dangerous would it be ? Jesus, why did everything have to be so complicated ?

Sean and Harry finished their conversation with the usual pleasantries but both had their minds elsewhere. Sean was trying to work out the next move and who should make it, whilst Harry was somewhere altogether more sinister. Had Billy Boyd left this mortal coil of his own volition or had he been pushed ? If he'd been pushed, why and by whom ? He had to admit he couldn't really

cope with any more at present so he and Sean had agreed to talk

the following day and both had gone back to their own thoughts,

two thousand miles apart but in situation they had never been

closer.

The flame flickered momentarily before it took hold. The orange ,

red and blue toyed easily with the cheap material fiercely seeking

something more worthy of its attention. The papers on the wall

began to yield almost as easily and then all was overtaken by the

discovery of fresh prey, liberally doused in petrol which teased the

flames to the point of abstraction before turning the cabin into an

intense inferno greedily feeding on its own substance.

The body would never be found - at least not recognisable as a

body. Sure, somebody could probably work out that the cabin

hadn't been empty but the identity of the poor unfortunate would keep several dentists in public service cheques for a very long time.

But then that was the point.

Slowly, but alas too fast; the adrenaline eased and the heat

subsided. The outside of the cabin was still recognisable but only

by someone who knew it real well whilst internally nothing

remained that wasn't at least lightly toasted.

In Washington, Sean and Harry's absence had not gone unnoticed,

the captain had covered their tracks, Gaynor had been taken into

custody and the department had carried on as close to normal as it

could. It was just more understaffed than usual.

Their absence had been relatively easy to hide, Sean had always

been an outsider so a transfer following the arrest of Gaynor was

seen as just rewards and a route back to somewhere close to the

big time whilst Harry had simply taken early retirement, bought a

boat and headed east , which if anything was rather too close to the

truth. Still, who was to know.

Since the timely demise of 'Billy' Boyd , Donnegan had been busy. It wasn't like he had a choice. Parkinson had made that clear enough. Up to now, he had turned up little on Sean and Terry but then as single people with few ties both were difficult to track. Donnegan already knew to his cost how Terry could disappear but both would keep and both were still vulnerable if only to each other. They would keep. Harry had been easier to track. Both Harry and Jean had extensive family ties and sooner or later someone had talked. He already knew where they had headed he just didn't have a firm fix but with an organisation that made the NYPD look like the Boy Scouts it wouldn't be long. He already had the beginnings of a plan and all the time the four of them were separated and in hiding 'the pipeline' could continue untroubled.. Donnegan had had the sense to have a contingency plan drawn up -'the pipeline' could be shut down relatively quickly and vehicles could always be transferred to other markets depending on which direction 'the heat' came from. Even now, he had allowed himself the luxury of marvelling at what a great idea 'the pipeline' had been. Michaels was none the wiser, the hole in the line had been filled by another, all the cops had was a small time thief and a delinquent manager who knew less then even he realised. Drugs and cars was nothing new and without Gaynor's briefcase there was no case. The local cops hadn't got it and with Boyd out of the picture and Mason believing Parkinson was one of the good guys things were still under control.

He had watched the cop's house for two weeks. He knew the routine, he knew the timing and he knew the woman better than the cop did. He had seen her dress and undress. He had admired the smooth contours of her body and he would again. The house would burn easily it was just a case of working out who would be in it at the time. He would like all four but more people meant more problems. But more people meant more fun .The woman would be easy and he would take his time. Kids were good but unpredictable.

The only real given was that the cop would die. Who would see it ,

who else would die were just details. Either way, the cop would die.

No matter where you are, who you are or how you live the normal

routine of everyday life will be your undoing. Nobody knew Harry

and Jean in Annapolis they were just another couple from the grey

brigade heading south for the winter and taking a boat on the

harbour. But they still needed food, the boat didn't run itself and

money is always money. Sean and Harry had spoken several times

since the first call . Never at the same time, never from the same

booth but one thing had remained constant. The papers had

steadfastly refused to report the demise of the biggest drug

smuggling operation in the northern hemisphere concentrating

instead on the 'Orioles' run to The World Series and the possibility

of a second term for Clinton, impeachment or no impeachment.

Initially they had decided to continue to lay low. They already knew

that the organisation was potentially vast and like the heads of the hydra it would need to be slain simultaneously. All Sean had been able to present at the senate house had been supposition , it would take time to build a case particularly when the full extent of the organisation was unknown and federal staff would need to work with local agencies but could only do so once their involvement had been disproved

Sean had already had cause to question their rapid departure. He was not prepared for a long time in hiding and whilst Harry and Jean had merely moved up their plans and chosen their second location Sean had plans to return to some sort of normal existence given the choice. Nobody spoke of Terry.

They had chosen to accept the death of 'Billy Boyd' as unfortunate and in truth they had little choice. Inwardly Harry was convinced otherwise but to speak his views would only serve to upset Jean and besides what could they do? Returning to Washington would be suicide. Approaching a second politician whose credentials they were unsure of would only serve to attract attention and the organisation had had plenty of time to regroup and dig in. They had accepted that their best hope rested with Simon Parkinson and the intervention of the British. He wasn't expecting the guys on Capitol Hill to like it but at least they would come in quick and clean. Till then they would just have to sit tight and Sean would have to find a way of supplementing the cash he had come away with.

Over the phone Harry had had a chance to reduce the levity of the situation this last point had prompted some interesting alternative careers for Sean who even as he hung up was contemplating the two last which had drawn belly laughs from them both and left Sean with tears of laughter running down his cheeks. Considering the situation they were in a career as a male model just seemed to conjure up all sorts of possibilities which given Sean's alcoholic history and sadly neglected body was never likely to threaten any of the regulars.

For Harry the bonhomie was not entirely forced. He missed Sean and knew that the last thing Sean needed was to be cast adrift again in a new place with no contacts and a liquor store just round

the corner. Montana might have been light years away

geographically but they had liquor stores just like everywhere else.

Sean needed people more than he knew and whilst Harry had

assumed that Terry had just drifted back into the life of a loner and

he and Jean had simply retired early, for Sean such dislocation was

not the wisest move and Harry knew how hard Sean had found it to

fit in at the DEA and how hard he had fallen after Terry.

The children ran carelessly across the road and dove in to the back

of the station wagon. News was noisily exchanged over the chaos

of reunion after a separation which had lasted less than a day but

which appeared worthy of a prolonged confinement. Amidst a hail

of questions, hugs and twinkies, crucial information was exchanged

in all directions and none of it was lost.

The scene was much like any other replayed a thousand times

across Middle America

Donnegan had always believed in redundancy. Not the sort where

people move on, the sort where you have two plans and not just

the one. He had two plans now.

The Pipeline : (8)

The cop would die first.

Donnegan needed to send a message in clear speech to Mason and the cop would do the job nicely. Once the message had gone out Parkinson could meet Mason , get the briefcase to 'help build the case' and then Mason and the others could be taken out. This was plan A. There was a plan B but Donnegan didn't think it would be needed. He had looked at it from all the angles and he couldn't see a losing hand. Parkinson had reacted well to the plan , 'the pipeline' was still intact with every prospect of remaining so and neither killing would be traceable to them for a number of reasons. (Donnegan had the sheriffs in his pocket, the drug dependent goons responsible would themselves only survive their victims by a matter of hours and the trail would be a sure-fire dead end) .

But first the cop would die.

This was terror, she had wondered how it felt, what it looked like, where it hit home. Terror is where you live. Everything, everyone you hold dear, threatened beyond endurance, toyed with before your very eyes and you, powerless in the extreme. She should have known. It wasn't the rogue driver at the lights or the drunk with the gun. All of this would be quick. It was instead the cold, calculated planning of somebody completely rational who knew exactly what they were doing. Somebody who knows your routine better than you do. Somebody who knows your child's name, their school, their friends and their father. Somebody who knows when you're home, when you're out and when you're vulnerable. Not just when you're vulnerable, but where you're vulnerable and who to. Someone who knows who can push the buttons and just how far to go. Somebody who knows it all and yet somebody who you don't know at all. Simple really.

She was terrified now. Not terrified she'd never get into a size ten

ever again, not terrified she'd forget to pay the milkman but ; cold

as steel, twist in the guts, these are my children, terrified. They

were her children. They were never meant to see any of this. It had

been so easy. She had come back from the bank just like she always

did. She had run a bath and gone back into the other room to

undress. She always had time for herself before the kids came back

. Time for herself before her man came back. The man waiting for

her had not been hers. He had watched and waited. She had

undressed. He had watched and waited. She had washed away the

stress of the day he had enjoyed every second. He had watched and

waited. When he had finished with her they had watched and

waited together ; she, in deep shock with the ruined remains of her

underwear hanging in tatters. Aware only of deep,deep pain and

sheer abject terror.

Chris would be first . She prayed class would go on longer, that she would linger longer over the latest gossip or some boy whom they would never meet. No child should see their mother like this.

The key in the lock brought her out of her reverie. He had heard it too.

The fear twisted in her gut and slithered out of her in a warm gush. She could hear it all so clearly. The thump of the bag on the floor, the trek to the fridge, the slurp from the carton , so often believed unseen, the foot on the stair. This was not Chris.

Luke, her first born, entered the room. The shock appeared momentarily on his face just before the reversed .45 crashed into his head. He slumped to the ground oblivious to the sickening crack of bone on floor and the soft, seeping blood that flowed from beneath his curls. She was torn. Horrified as her son hit the floor and yet secretly overjoyed that it had not been Chris for her suffering would surely have lasted much longer.

Silently, she wept. Silently she thanked God for the unseen friend who had delayed her daughter.

For Sean, nothing was ever easy. He couldn't even flee for his life without bringing in his very own set of extra traumas. Even now as a romantic hero-in-hiding his problems were heightened by the simple yet ridiculous status of not having enough shorts to get through the time it would take to sort out his supply lines. Whilst jumping into the Camaro and heading out of town might have looked good as the final scene for a 'Dirty Harry' movie , in reality it just meant that he had driven too far, too soon and without any thought for his own survival beyond the minimal time it would take the Right Honourable Simon Parkinson to bring down the wrath of God on the wrong doers. Only that just wasn't happening.

Sure, he knew enough to realise that Steve Gaynor had been well in over his head and that the system that revolved around the plant was pretty sophisticated but how long was it going to take the feds to sort it out ? A coupla days at most ? Steve, Terry, Harry and Jean

had been in hiding for nearly three weeks. In that time Billy Boy

Boyd had met what looked like a perfectly peaceful end and the

papers had resolutely refused to print any story that came even

remotely close to an industrial / drugs cartel .So what the hell was

going on ?

Sean knew damn well. Sweet FA. If he was honest with himself he

had known for some time that nothing was happening. He had seen

through Harry's bravado and he knew that the danger they faced

was still very real. If anything it was worse. The bare bones of the

plot had been laid bare and become public knowledge. Or so he had

hoped. But Billy Boy had gone to meet his maker and maybe, just

maybe, the whole bloody mess was still just between the three of

them. For Sean the choices were easy. Sooner or later he had to go

back. He simply didn't have enough resources to hole up in

Montana until something happened. If nothing happened he could

no more start afresh here than he could swim backstroke to the moon. (Things were going well weren't they ?) He was the only

person the authorities knew , he couldn't ask Harry to put his life at

risk and Terry was long gone. Why did it always come down to him?

Like the man said , sooner or later he would have to go back. He

just didn't know when or how. His place would be a complete no-go

area and with Harry gone as well, his most obvious bolt holes were

already knackered. (This plan just got better and better) The

Camaro was probably not a good idea either, both Parkinson and

Boyd had seen it so at best he was looking at an anonymous bus

trip covering two thousand miles back to Washington where he had

nowhere to stay. (peachy - just peachy)

Harry knew Sean would go back. It was obvious. Despite, the old-

timer-waiting-out-his-pension tag Harry still knew how many beans

made five and last time he'd looked it was still five. Three weeks

was three weeks in anybody's language. It didn't matter who they

were using the good guys could have shipped in the SAS on a slow boat from Blighty and it should still have been all over by now. Even

the feds didn't move this slow. Harry also knew that Sean would be

well on his way to a major guilt trip by now. He would be blaming

himself for the lack of action and once he had had enough bourbon

he would do something that was just plain stupid.

If Sean had needed anything to convince him about the need to

head back to Washington. The next days' headlines were just the

ticket. All the major papers carried horrific pictures of the murder

of a east coast police captain and his family who had all burned

inside their house without any alarm being raised until it was too

late. The details were sketchy but there were clearly questions

being raised over the deaths. Why had all the family been together

in the one room ? How come they were all sitting on hard chairs

upstairs ? There was little evidence of clothing on the mother and

female children.

Sean didn't need a picture. The names were enough. Message received and understood.

The call from Harry wasn't long in coming. The papers in Annapolis had been full of it. They had put forward several theories all of which were so far from the mark it was laughable. The possibility of police corruption had made Harry's hackles rise and the killings had even been linked to the disappearance of Sean and Harry with dirt being dredged out of their files to justify the claims. (peachy - just peachy) Sean was portrayed as 'inherently insubordinate' who had been passed over too many times whilst Harry was depicted as his weak-willed partner who had just wanted to get back at the establishment. There was just enough detail to make it believable but only just. Either way, it wasn't going to help their case. Sure enough, in a couple of days the whole story would blow over, but by then it would be too late. Even if Harry and Sean had comtemplated going back for help, they were on their own now.

There was no doubt now. Sean would come. But best to make sure.

Friday was Friday , same as ever the whole world over. No more work, time for shopping , the children and the day of rest which never quite made it.

Breakfast broke in the Carpenter household like a low yield atomic explosion - plenty of noise but not too much devastation. To an outsider all appeared strictly choreographed with subtle moves defining pecking order and bathroom preferences. To an insider it was just the normal everyday mayhem of middle America. Alarms and dog walking; showers and shaving; clothes and make-up. The routine was comforting and frustrating. Every house knows it.

Waffles and toast; cereal and coffee; juice and bagels.

Bourbon and more bourbon. Jack Daniels was here when we went to bed and he's here when we wake up. You couldn't buy commitment like that. Beats a wife anyday. No shave, no shower , no family, no friends, in the middle of fuckin' nowhere. Ain't life grand

Work and school; bus and train, station wagon. He had seen it all before. Not here, not this neighbourhood but the result could be the same. White, not black but the bitch was still worth looking at , two kids or not. They tumbled into the station wagon, a riot of school books and dogs.

No change of clothes, no breakfast. No real clue of what the hell to do. Surely even Harry could see that it was all smoke and mirrors ? Nowhere to go, except back to see good ol' Jack. He could probably put us up for a couple more days.

The black Starion mirrored every move the station wagon made but in truth he knew the journey better than she did. Left at the lights, left lane and peel left after the expressway. Shit, he could do it in his sleep. The school buses, the kids, the cars. Last day - thank god its Friday. Poets day, piss off early, tomorrow's Saturday. Piss of early, and never see your parents again.

Kids at school. Wife at the mall. Hubby at work. Christ, how easy could they make it.

No change of clothes, no breakfast. Not a real clue of what the hell to do. Nowhere to go, except back to see good ol' Jack. He could probably put us up for a couple more days.

" Your Dad's been held up at work, asked me to pick you up"
Shit - like shooting rats in a barrel.

Rats in a barrel

Sean looked like shit. A week in the same clothes had taken the edge off what Harry chose to call 'his rugged appeal'. Sean knew it was bullshit. His rugged appeal had headed south around the same time as his marriage. Self pity of biblical proportions and a liberal dose of Uncle Jack had completed the job. Harry had seen it all before - too many times. Jesus, Sean could beat himself up better than any thug he had ever had the misfortune to meet. A decent

right hand was just no match for a broken marriage, kids he'd never

had and ten years of self pity. Absolutely no contest.

This may have been Montana but it might just have well have been

Sean's apartment in town. It had just taken him longer to get there.

It made a pretty picture. The captain was long gone. Billy Boyd was

long gone. The pipeline was, in all probability, still completely intact

and Sean looked like shit and probably felt worse.

Sean picked himself up as Harry came through the door. The room

said more than Sean could. The debris from three weeks in exile

was scattered around the room . No corner had remained

untouched. There were at least two things that Sean was really

good at, police work and by God, he could go on a bender with the

best of them.

By the time Sean had showered and at least some of his senses had

returned Harry had got some coffee on and started to sort out the room. Sean was still at least four senses short but he knew enough to shut up and take his medicine.

Only Jean knew the number and she would never phone. Harry sat down heavily as the colour washed out of him. He put his head in his hands and swore for what Sean believed was very possibly the first time in his life. The phone went dead and Harry crashed it into the cradle.

"Sit down Sean"

Harry's voice was thick with emotion, or was it hatred. (after all these years you still can't tell the difference can you, you useless smuck) . Sean stood motionless. His body had no idea what messages his brain was trying to push through and it had less idea how to put them into action.

"For Chrissakes sit down , they've got Jean ....and they've got the kids".

Harry fell so far forward Sean went to steady him but Harry braced himself against the dresser.

"Who's fuckin kids ?"

"How in God's name did they find your kids, even you don't know where they are !".

The humour was lost on Harry and Sean instantly regretted it .

"They've got Fay's kids!"

"Fay's kids !"

Sean slumped onto the bed, next to Harry as their situation hit him full in the face. It hurt more than any physical blow. Harry had stayed in touch with Fay long after they had gone their separate ways if only to make sure she was ok and just in case there was any hope of a reconciliation sometime in the future. (Yeah right) . Harry had known that Fay had married again and that there had been children but after her marriage Harry had reasoned, rightly as it turned out, that he was just another reminder of Sean and that he should fade into the background.

"Why Fay's kids ? "

"What the hell does that matter ? . Its for real. They sent hair this morning. Just thank God Fay hasn't got a clue where you are."

Sean had never even met Fay's kids. Christ he hadn't seen Fay in more than ten years . Still thought about her everyday, but hey who was counting.

"What do they want ?

"What the hell do you think they want ?.They want you, me and the briefcase."

"But we haven't got the briefcase"

"I know that and you know that, but they don't and all the time Jean isn't forced to tell them we still have a chance. Now shut the fuck up, right now you're worse than useless"

Sean may have been four sheets to the wind but he knew when to shut up. Harry was clearly getting to like the 'f' word and Sean wasn't about to start questioning him despite the fact that he had little or no idea what the hell was going on. (if there had been a plan , it had all gone to hell in a hand basket now) The coffee was starting to revive him but as more of his senses came on line so the true reality of the situation started to emerge from the haze. It wasn't a pretty picture.

They had waited for Harry to leave Jean before moving on her and plans for the kids' abduction must have been drawn up straight after the meeting. But who was pulling the strings? Sean found it hard to credit Billy Boyd with anything more than a safe seat and a nice line in southern hospitality, which meant all of this was down to Parkinson in which case you could forget about any cavalry turning up anytime soon.

They had a couple of hours before the next phone call was due so they had some time. Harry put it to good use.

He had to admire whoever was behind the scenes. Taking Jean alone would never have guaranteed Sean's return and as much as Harry wanted to believe he was of some value to them he knew they wanted Sean. Taking Fay's kids had hit Sean where he lived.

Harry would come back because of Jean, Sean would come back because of Fay. Whatever possessed them to believe that a couple of broken down cops could take down the sort of organisation that could have been shifting heroin in industrial quantities since the plant had opened. Jesus, who did they think they were kidding ? There wasn't going to be any cavalry, no press, no heroes, nothing changes. Neat, real neat.

There was some good news. Terry was obviously in the clear. Using Terry to get to Sean would have been much simpler so Harry reckoned it was safe to assume that Terry was safe. If Terry was safe then the briefcase was safe. (at least that part of the plan had worked) . But what happened now ? Harry wasn't sure whether he and Sean had any cards left to play, and even if they had, every play they had made so far had been one step behind the game. Harry needed Sean, back, and firing on all cylinders and he needed him now.

The Pipeline : (9)

Even without Sean it didn't take a genius to work out that their

options were just a little on the limited side. It may have been a

selection, but it wasn't exactly a choice. With Parkinson holding all

the aces they had to go back. They could go with the briefcase (but

they needed Terry back for that and Harry wasn't sure Sean would

ever be ready to see Terry again) and hope that Parkinson was a

man of his word (yeah , right); they could go without the briefcase

and tough it out; they could go to the FBI, but with the children

being held this was never going to be an option or they could just

run like hell.

Sean had to admit that he liked the sound of the last one. Hell, he

didn't owe Fay any favours - he hated children anyway (didn't he ?),

and Harry could do without Jean. Yeah sure he could. Losing Jean

would be like losing his right arm and he knew it and Sean already

knew they had plenty of options but only one choice. They just had to make sure they held at least a couple of jokers. (you rang m'lord)

.

They did have a couple of advantages. They knew the city and they had something, or Parkinson thought they had something, that he wanted real bad. They could call the shots, or at least a few of them. All they had to do was get to Jean and the kids before Parkinson realised that the briefcase they held was useless. (piece of cake). Before the next call they had worked out where they wanted the 'exchange' to take place and who would be there. Sean reckoned that as an outsider Parkinson would have little knowledge of the city but he would have to be there. He wasn't about to let the briefcase out of his sight and he wouldn't trust it to one of his henchmen. However, trying to dictate who was to be there on both sides was never going to be easy. Even if he got agreement he knew damn well that Parkinson was never going to honour any bargain he made with Sean.

Even if you knew the city, downtown D.C. wasn't a place for the faint hearted. As the rest of the city had basked in its status as the federal capital and taken tourist dollars like it was going out of fashion the downtown area had basked in its own success as the murder capital of the USA. Rather than put social programmes in place to support the urban poor the city had become increasingly segregated until now the dichotomy between rich and poor had become clear for all to see. Washington could boast some of the most expensive real estate in the world and yet just a matter of a few blocks from the Smithsonian and the White House walking was a life threatening exercise. The city had adopted a policy of 'containment'. which meant even the poor were moving out. The less fortunate and those sleeping rough had found sprinkler systems installed to prevent sleeping in the parks, 'armed response' security guards protecting doorways and businesses whilst the beautiful people of D.C. had simply created walled and patrolled private ghettos of their own where they imprisoned themselves far beyond the reality of urban living.

This would be where the 'exchange' would take place. Sean and Harry had intimate local knowledge, knew where was safe and where was not. They could get in and get out quick and if need be they could hole up with Jean and the kids until Parkinson either gave up the chase or found himself somewhere he shouldn't be. Either way, the streets would be their ally and right now Sean and Harry needed all the allies they could get. Harry would take the call. Harry had argued that he could handle it no problem and that he was less emotional than Sean. Sean had countered with the fact that Jean's involvement made Harry just as emotional as he was but ultimately they both knew that Parkinson knew too much about Sean already and would know just which buttons to press to make him lose his cool. Sean doubted whether Harry could stay dispassionate but he knew damn well that he couldn't.

The call was on time. Despite the usual electronic trickery Sean was sure he could detect the clipped British accent beneath the disguise. Sean thought back to the last time they had spoken and how much faith he had put in this one man. He silently scolded himself for his poor judgement. Parkinson was trying to dictate the terms but his knowledge was limited. Sean could make out several other voices with Parkinson's. Sean was sure that Michaels would be there and he found it hard to believe that his time on the track was even part of his current existence. Michaels' voice brought the memories and pain flooding back. Harry was stalling, desperate to have proof that Jean was still alive. Parkinson wasn't keen to play ball but Harry cut across him roughly, they were on his turf now; "For Chrissakes we're out here on our own. What difference does it make how long you stay on the phone ? Its not like we can track you, you've made damn sure that we're alone so shut the fuck up and let me speak to my wife".

Sean was seeing a new side to Harry, one in which the 'f' word was an integral part of his vocabulary and one where he didn't take any shit from anybody. Not least from some dope-trafficking fuckwit who was holding his wife.

The phone went dead.

(OK, so they want to play hardball)

Two minutes later the phone rang again. Harry had to physically restrain himself from grabbing it up at the first ring and he stopped Sean from doing likewise. Harry allowed it to ring five times before he picked it up.

"Now put Jean on and stop screwing around"

Harry knew he was in no position to demand anything but suddenly Jean's voice came over the line.

Harry managed to hang together long enough to agree a location with Michaels, although it was obvious Parkinson was pulling the strings. Michaels hadn't accepted their first choice but the second location had been agreed and if truth be told Harry had Sean had deliberately presented their choices of location in reverse order so they were happy with the outcome. It would be a simple exchange. Sean and Harry would get Jean and the kids . Parkinson would get Gaynor's briefcase which held all the evidence to blow the case wide open. Sean and Harry had managed to avoid one key fact. Gaynor's briefcase was currently somewhere in Toronto with Terry. But hey, anyone could make a mistake.

Sean had been making mistakes ever since he could remember. Wrong woman, wrong job, wrong time, wrong drink. Sean had been screwing it up for the best part of twenty years. Sooner or later, the man calls 'time'. Sean had vowed it many times before but this time he meant it. Win, lose or draw it had to be the wagon. If everything went wrong it was hardly going to matter anyway.

Harry knew that Sean had seen better days and 'the rugged charm' had taken one too many beatings but they needed to be together on this one and Harry knew if the shit hit the fan, he could still count on Sean. If he was honest, Harry also knew that talking to

Jean had damn near pushed him over the limit. Right then he would have agreed to just about anything just to keep her talking on the line never mind to actually see her again. At that moment he would have gladly sold out the children, Terry, the briefcase, Sean, Father Christmas, Mother Theresa, anything. Right now they made a good team.

They had seven days. Parkinson wouldn't give them a day longer and whilst Harry knew they needed time to prepare, the sooner this was all over the better he would feel.

Harry thanked God for the Camaro. Whilst as transport it was about as cool as borrowing your Dad's car, as a mobile arsenal it had few peers. Whilst the thing handled like a pig on ice; there were definite compensations. The boot yielded nearly four hundred rounds of assorted ammunition most of which was standard issue, but some of which was not; a variety of weapons, most of which Harry didn't want to know where they came from and a couple of suits of body armour which would not have looked out of place on your local

SWAT team. Given Sean's propensity for danger, most of it had never been used.

What they needed now was an edge and the location and the guns would give it to them. Sean however had saved the best till last. As they surveyed their mounting arsenal, now laid out neatly on the hotel room floor, Sean produced the piece de resistance. From under the Camaro's rear seat he pulled a dark green gun bag which he handled with almost reverential care. Only when they were both back in the room and the door locked did he reveal its contents. He drew the zip back slowly and the unmistakable smell of gun oil drifted into the room. Sean slowly reached in and drew out what appeared to be a rifle . Harry had been hoping for an Abrams or at least a Chieftain tank so his sense of anti climax was palpable as Sean drew out the weapon and placed it in the floor. Clearly, Harry was missing something.

"Ok , so you've got a rifle. Its rate of fire is crap, it s range is probably crap and you'd have to be Jake the Peg to conceal it.

Sean was not amused. He began taking the rifle apart and then oiling it piece by piece. Judging by his actions he could do this with his eyes closed. With a similar level of care he explained to Harry that sure , it looked like a rifle and indeed it was rifle. But it was a UK sniper rifle and as such it could kill a man at a 1000 yards. The rifle was dark green with a standard bolt action but there its similarity with other rifles ended. It was long barrelled and very smooth with a stock which fitted the hand like no other and which could make even the most untutored amateur a deadly killing machine at four hundred yards. The action was smooth and precise and although it fired standard NATO rounds and did without delicate sights, it had been a revelation in the Gulf. With the sort of skill which Sean could only dream about it could take out a head-sized target from a mile and a half. Sean reckoned 500 yards would be all that they would need. They had their edge. Now all they had to worry about was transporting enough ordnance to supply a small army half way across America.

Seven days to travel half way across America in ageing Camaro laden with ammunition was going to tax even someone with Sean's advanced driving skills. They would spell each other at the wheel and aim to get back to Washington in five days to give them a couple of days to set up and check out their escape routes. Even then what they would really need would be a couple of days sleep. Harry had to admit that he still wasn't convinced. If he and Sean both had to be at the handover, who would use the rifle ? If they started shooting from 500 yards away Parkinson would simply start killing the children until they came out of hiding. Harry would still rather have had an Abrams.

In five days and four nights Sean and Harry had learned a great deal. About the Camaro, about each other and about themselves. Harry knew that he would never , but never sleep in a car again.

Sean knew that he would never drive with Harry again and they both knew what they really needed was a miracle.

They had made good time and had found a cheap hotel which would be their base. They had slept and eaten well , although Sean's permanent diet of burgers, hot dogs and root beer had never appealed to Harry but they were just about ready.

Sean reckoned now was about as good a time as any to show Harry the closest thing he had to a miracle. The two pieces of kit he had left in the Camaro and not shown him in Montana. As they headed back to the hotel the evening before the handover Sean delved deep into his inside pocket and placed a short, dark green tube on Harry's palm. He reached into the other side of his jacket and placed a larger, shorter tube in Harry's other hand. Harry looked questioningly at Sean and then slowly opened the first case. The good news was the rifle had a silencer but at the second case Harry looked bemused. He had always assumed the rifle had some form of sights so he failed to grasp the significance of Sean's latest toy. They climbed to their room and Sean attached both pieces of kit to the rifle. He focussed the sights and then invited Harry to take a look.

Despite the fact that it was very late; through the sight the street glowed with an eary green light. Harry could easily pick out all the detail of the city tableau beneath them. Now they had their edge and Harry could believe in it.

Sean had been spread-eagled across the rooftop for nearly half an hour. They had been in place for the best part of two hours before the agreed meeting time and Sean had surveyed every inch of the disused lot beneath him. The ground was covered roughly two blocks and , once upon a time, had been a warehouse for the local sweat shops. Sean knew every inch of it and as the time had ticked slowly by he had watched each one of Parkinson's men take up a position well within the capability of the rifle that he now held in his grasp. He could take any or all of them anytime he wanted.

Unlike Sean Harry had had little to occupy his mind. There are only so many ways you can clean and reassemble a Colt. Harry knew them all. He had been pacing for the last half hour. The briefcase, such as it was, was filled with menus from a deli across the street and between them Harry and Sean carried more than eight weapons and nearly four hundred rounds of ammunition. If it came down to a foot race they were knackered.

The plan, like all good plans, was simple. It might not work, but at least it was simple.

Sean picked out the furthest man. The sight glowed green in the soft light of dusk and Sean was able to pick out every detail of the life he was about to take. The guy was a little overweight, spent too much time behind the wheel and didn't take enough exercise. He was probably headed for a heart attack before he was forty. Hell, Sean was doing him a favour.

Sean placed the cross hairs on the guy's chest and exhaled slowly.

He could take him any time he wanted, but not yet. Sean and Harry

had watched the routine. The goons were calling in every fifteen

minutes and there was still a half hour till the rendez-vous. Harry

was watching the back . They waited. The minutes ticked past

slowly as Sean waited to start the killing. It had been a long time

and even then he'd never been that good at it. Sean watched the

goon call in for what would be the last time. Slowly he replaced the

cross hairs over the guy's chest , exhaled and squeezed the trigger.

The rifle made a small coughing noise and through the sights Sean

watched him go down. Sean immediately swung the rifle through

180 degrees and sighted on the second guy. He was nearly half a

mile away but he wouldn't be making another call either. In a little

over twenty seconds Sean had dramatically reduced the odds

against them and who was to know ?

Quickly, he dismantled the rifle and joined Harry with the briefcase.

They climbed into the Camaro and cruised into the lot. The next part of the plan wasn't quite so straightforward. Parkinson had underestimated their firepower but close to the rifle would count for nothing. Now, it was all about bluff.

Parkinson, Donnegan and Michaels had set up shop at the far end of the lot. They were covered on three sides by vehicles. Sean could see a dark sided Chrysler Voyager and a couple of Jeeps. The irony wasn't lost on Sean. Sean had always known that Parkinson had had no intention of only bringing two aides and although Sean had done his best to even things up, they were still outnumbered.

Harry and Sean drove slowly into what in effect had become a corral. If the fourth side closed behind them, the were lost. Sean swung the car so that it was facing back out the way they had come, stopped and they got out slowly. Sean then let Harry pull out a couple of yards ahead of him and Sean turned to check their escape route. It would all be in the timing.

"Where's my wife"

Harry had decided to take the initiative and he wasn't about to take any crap from Parkinson, not today.

"We want the briefcase , pure and simple. You can have your wife, and the kids, nobody gets hurt. Nobody does anything stupid."

Donnegan, not Parkinson, was conducting affairs. Sean decided that was not a good thing.

"You start the people, I'll bring the briefcase. I'll leave it halfway, you come and get it, once the women are clear."

"You seem to forget Mr. Mason you are in no position to make demands. Michaels, - you remember Mr Michaels don't you Sean ? - will come out to meet you and take the briefcase .

Sean knew this was as good as he was going to get. The sight of Jean getting out of the Voyager was enough to send Harry weak at the knees . She looked okay and the kids looked unharmed - but it was a helluva group to move across no-man's land. Harry looked at Sean and started walking towards Donnegan. Donnegan started the group towards Sean. Sean had got a good deal. Parkinson could

have tried to swap half the hostages whilst he checked the papers,
at least this way they had a chance. At the half way point Harry put
the briefcase down. Having Michaels pick it up would give them
another few seconds. The group kept walking. Harry started to
retrace his steps, slowly and walking backwards. The briefcase had
a combination. Michaels was spinning the tumblers, Jean was
nearly to Sean, Harry was screening the kids. Michaels flicked the
locks and for what seemed like an eternity he stared down in
disbelief. He was no genius but he knew this wasn't part of the deal.
As he dropped the case, Parkinson and his other goons started to
take a real interest and reached for whatever weapons they had to
hand. Jean was with Sean , he pushed roughly into the Camaro. The
kids were with Harry and they were nearly at the car. Sean drew the
nine millimetre from his waistband, took careful aim at Michaels
and squeezed. Even now time was running in 'long play' , Michaels
went down and Sean rushed to shepherd the kids in to Camaro.
Next to him the screen of the Camaro exploded as a heavy calibre

shell buried itself in the dashboard. The kids were in the car, Sean and Harry were standing side by side squeezing off shots like the last stand of Butch and Sundance. This might work. With Harry covering him Sean dove for the Camaro and shoved it in gear. The ancient transmission whined at his heavy handedness but slammed into gear and the car hurtled forward as Sean buried his foot in the carpet. As he looked up he saw Harry take a shot in the shoulder and behind him Jean screamed. It still might work. Harry fell rather then jumped in to the car and Sean aimed for the far end of the lot with screams all around him and bullets burying themselves in the Camaro like some demented side show game. The blasts were all around and Parkinson wasn't just using handguns. The crack of rifle fire was sending heavy calibre bullets in to the engine bay and Sean knew the Camaro wasn't built to take this kind of punishment. If they could clear the lot, they could still make it.

They weren't going to clear the lot. In front of the wheezing Camaro Sean saw two figures stand to face the car . Both held military style

M16 which they were emptying into the Camaro. The tyres blew

out in near perfect unison and Sean struggled to control two tons of

America's finest riding on its wheels. They weren't going to make it

and they didn't have anything to bargain with . They would be lucky

if Parkinson didn't simply beat out the location of the real briefcase

and kill someone for everyday that it took to get it here. Sean

swung the wheel hard over and threw himself out of the door. As

he came upright behind the rear of the car he fired two shots taking

out the bastards with the M16 and buying them a little more time.

In the lot, Parkinson and Donnegan had both grabbed a Jeep and

were hurtling towards the stricken Camaro. Sean fired continually

till the clip was empty, threw down the pistol and reached behind

the seat for the Uzi stowed in the lining. Bullets flew from its muzzle

but they were never going to stop the Jeeps now bearing down on

the Camaro like metallic dinosaurs sensing fresh meat. Donnegan's

Jeep hit the Camaro square in the side just behind the door, The car

jumped back at the impact and metal crumpled vividly. Sean and

Harry knew that was it. They threw down their guns and stood up slowly. Parkinson brought his Jeep to a standstill sliding delicately in to the front wing of the Camaro which was now nothing more than an expensive paperweight. Parkinson got out, walked to Sean and head butted him viciously. "Now, Mr Mason, perhaps we could stop pratting about"

Sean spat. It was more a reflex to the blood running in to his mouth but it was better than any words he could muster.

This wasn't in the plan. In as little over twenty minutes since Sean had started taking out the Parkinson sentinels the bottom had fallen out of Sean's world. Far from driving off into the sunset with a full set of hostages and his trusty companion at his side he was bloodied, bruised and all he had accomplished was to add to the number of hostages by a factor of two and convince Parkinson that he was little more than a lowly paid cowboy. Harry had been shot in the shoulder, the Camaro was a pile of scrap and there was even less chance of any cavalry turning up anytime soon. The pipeline was still sending thousands of dollars worth of Cherokee into Europe along with millions of pounds of heroin. Nice one.

In truth, the mayhem had finished almost as quickly as it started . Although Sean was convinced bullets had been flying for the best part of a fortnight the actual firefight had lasted less than two minutes. Their capture had followed shortly after with the only further violence being visited on Sean when Parkinson realised the extent of his losses. Although Sean had allowed himself a touch of pride it had cost him a severe beating. Jean had done her best to sort out his wounds but if truth be told the rugged charm had all but been replaced by ugly bruising.

They had little choice now but to deliver the real briefcase and hope that Parkinson would see little point in killing them but given the amount that they now knew about his operation Harry could see no way they would be allowed to live.

———————————————————————————————————

The Pipeline : (10)

Harry now had little choice but to bring Terry into play. He had known where she was headed all along but he had hoped that she would make it scot free. That just wasn't going to happen now. Peter and Fay had already been lead a merry dance by Parkinson's men and no doubt they would be none too impressed when she realised how Harry and Sean had gambled with the lives of their children . What had seemed like a perfectly viable plan two hours ago had been shown to be nothing more than the adolescent musings of a couple of over confident has beens.

Parkinson now wanted all the players in clear sight. Fay and Peter were desperate to see Terry and more importantly the briefcase and Parkinson didn't want anymore surprises. Harry reckoned they were all out of surprises anyway. Harry picked up the phone and called her. The plan was easy. Bring the briefcase now. No police, no heroes, no drama.

So this was Terry. She should have known. Terry had 'Sean' written

all over her . Sean always made the same mistakes, bless him.

Always confident, breezy women who then scared the hell out of

him when they behaved in a confident and breezy way. Looking at

Terry was like looking at herself, only she had to admit - Terry was

at least five years younger and clearly had never had children.

Fay had deliberately cut herself off from Sean and she had tried to

build a new life without him. If only he knew how many times she

had reached for the phone. You can' t go back. Eventually, she had

managed to move on enough to contemplate another relationship

and she knew Peter was good and strong and honest and her

mother had said she needed a 'good'un' but he wasn't Sean and he

never would be.

She had tried to work out Sean's attraction if only so she could

avoid it in the future but she just knew that ultimately he had been

'the one' . When it was the real thing it never came down to a smile or a word ; the way they filled their jeans or how they ordered drinks , it was just supposed to be this way - until somebody fucked it up. He had never valued himself enough to realise that he was all that any sane woman could ask for. She had tried to make it work to the point where there was very little left of the real Fay but she had just hoped against hope that he would realise that she loved him and that that would never change. It still hadn't changed. Even now she loved him still.

Terry was tall and polite but this was never going to be easy. Ex-wife and current (ex ?) lover was never going to work for long. Perhaps they could survive long enough on pleasantries to sort out this mess. They probably had enough in common to make this work. If nothing else they were both petrified. Fay just wanted her children back and she could see that Terry was desperate to see Sean again whether she chose to admit it or not. Fay wanted Sean to survive but she wasn't sure whether seeing him again would be a good idea. She could worry about that later.

Fay wasn't sure how it had come to this. The events of the last month had seemed to happen like some bizarre computer game running at the wrong speed. Characters had no identity and just around the next corner was either your best friend or your worst nightmare (Peter meeting Sean - was that her worst nightmare?) . Somebody, somewhere probably had some sort of game plan but it sure as shit wasn't her.

It had been nearly ten years since she had seen Sean and she had wiped much of the memory away long ago. Their last meeting had been cordial in the extreme- both of them had known what it meant but neither had had any idea how much real pain would be involved. By then she had just wanted out. She hadn't really wanted out even then, it had just turned out that way. A train she couldn't get off. She had heard Sean had moved to the DEA and she had wished him well. Secretly she had always known that she had hurt him bad but what else could she have done. You can't love somebody if they won't let you. How can you love somebody if they don't really like themselves? It just becomes a battle to keep up the pretence of bullet-proof confidence and how many people do you know with bullet-proof confidence ?

She and Peter had built a good life. They had had two wonderful children and she had found other diversions in the local community and a small business that she had started with a small legacy left by her mother. It wasn't the excitement she believed she would have had with Sean but one self destruct was enough for anybody.

Her nemesis had come, not with the four horsemen of the apocalypse, not with fire, famine and plague but with the simple abduction of her children because someone she hadn't seen for more than a decade had got in way over his head.

If this was going to be hard for her, Fay realised that Peter was going to feel like it was Christmas and Thanksgiving rolled into one. He wanted his children back. He had no idea why they had been taken - marketing guys just didn't generate that much hatred. Close

- but not quite. Sure, he knew that Fay had had a life before he had

met her. Jeez, who didn't come with some sort of baggage ? But

this was different. Bumping into an ex by chance was fair enough so

long as they kept their distance and respected your life. This was

well beyond that. Bits of hair through the post, tapes of their

children begging for them to come, all because Fay had slept with

some sort of wacko. Now, to top it all some blast from-the-past bird

needed their help, and worse still they needed her . Yeah, this was

going to be a real doosie.

He wasn't stupid. He had always known that Fay had never had a

grand passion. He was a nice steady guy. He had never tried out for

the Mariners, the police had never been a career option and as for

the DEA , it was a part of life he had tried to shield his family from.

He was struggling to understand what the hell was happening.

Suddenly it wasn't about his children anymore it was about Terry,

Fay and Sean. It didn't take a genius to work out that Fay still

carried a torch for Sean. He had come to terms with it a long time ago, but then he hadn't figured on him putting in a guest appearance anytime soon.

All Fay really wanted to do was to slap Terry hard across the face and tell her to get the hell out of their lives, but the hell of it was if they couldn't work together then she would never see her children again. It was simple really. She was desperate to ask her about Sean. How was he ? Had he changed ? She wasn't sure if she really wanted to know, but she couldn't leave it. If they had had sex, was it better or worse than when she had been with Sean ? Had he cried, or was that only with her ?

Peter walked casually into the room, he had to meet her sooner or later. He had heard voices and now was as good as time as any. However, nothing that Fay had said to him had prepared him for the scene that greeted him as he entered the kitchen. Terry was quite simply, stunning. Sure the strain of the last few days had taken their tole on her but it was going to take a little more than a couple of dark circles to dim what was an extraordinary beauty. He was already out of his depth. He could handle the pleasantries easy enough but working closely with this woman was going to be harder than he had realised. Her aroma filled the room and Peter was conscious of this woman as he had never been conscious of any woman before Fay or since. Even here, with the piles of shit he had heaped on their lives, Peter had a grudging admiration for Sean. If you judged a man by the women in his life, Sean was a god.

"Suppose you tell us what this is all about"

Yeah right, like it was that easy. Terry had no idea where to start. Walking into somebody's house and telling them you're the reason their kids have been taken was not exactly the best starting point for a friendship. Plus, she was already picking up signs from Peter that friendship may not be the end of it. Like all she needed was another man right now !

Terry sat down, and started at the beginning. By the time she had finished Peter and Fay were sitting in what can only be called a rapt silence. To an outsider the whole thing sounded like 'Desmond

Bagley-on-speed' but it had been her life for the last four months. In truth, most of the shit of her life had been leading to this for the last five years. At least she had their attention.

The whole story had taken the best part of four hours and a bottle of Remy Martin to recount. Peter now found it difficult to gauge the reaction to all that Terry had been saying. Fay was clearly off balance. As far as he knew she had neither seen nor heard from Sean in nearly ten years and yet the latest twist to his life had had a profound effect on her own. Peter no longer trusted himself with Terry . The combined effects of the shock, the brandy and her very presence was enough to let him know that like Sean, he too was now in well over his head. Terry on the other hand was a picture of composure. If Peter had been prepared to let his mind run away Terry was way beyond any form of escape. The telling of her tale had gone some way to releasing some of her own demons and besides looking tired she appeared ready to face whatever the consequences of her actions had brought her.

In truth, if Sean , Harry , Jean and the children were to survive the next forty eight hours they had to work together and they had to start now. The story of the first botched handover had brought tears to the eyes of Terry and Fay although much of the detail was missing. The upshot of it all was that Sean and Harry had now joined the children as hostages and Parkinson now wanted the briefcase pure and simple. No heroes, no police, no drama.

"Jesus, you gels sure know how to find a whole pile of trouble." Terry and Peter were shocked at the intrusion. They had figured they were alone with Fay but the entry of a tall suited stranger into the farmhouse had added just the right note of surprise to crown Terry's story.

"Coffee would be good"

Fay automatically turned to the stove before stopping abruptly and turning back to the man in her kitchen.

"Just who the hell do you think you are ?"

"I know who I am m'am ,its you people who seem to believe that you're God's gift to law enforcement ".

It had taken the team nearly three months to track Terry and to be sure that no one was doing like wise. They had kept a watching brief but now that the affair had resulted in four, possibly six, deaths they had little option but to act. They couldn't prove the death of Billy Boyd had been anything other than routine but once the captain's family had been killed the federal law enforcement agencies had had their interest piqued. Parrish had been brought onto the case a little over two months ago and they had been tracking Terry, Harry and Jean for some time. They had lost sight of Harry once he went to meet Sean but they had been well aware of Jean's abduction although they had had little choice but to see where it lead. Parrish wasn't too pleased over that one. The kidnapping of Fay's children had come right out of left field only serving to complicate matters and making Parrish's job a whole lot harder.

" So where do we go from here ?"

It was Peter who broke the silence. His feelings of impotence had subsided somewhat. He no longer felt he was taking on the entire east coast mafia and with Parrish to deflect some of Terry's attraction he was beginning to feel that he might just make it through the next forty eight hours with his marriage intact and his family still together. It would be close but he thought he could pull it off.

The tall suit introduced himself as John Parrish. He was not alone. As the coffee came out two more cars arrived and more suits came into the farmhouse. In theory the briefcase was the centre of attention, although in reality it was running a poor second to Terry.

Peter didn't give a shit about the briefcase, he just wanted his kids

back. Coffee and biscuits was all very well but this wasn't a local

meeting of the WI. Six people had been killed already and these

guys were acting like it was some sort of garden party. The

briefcase was the key. He had no idea of the protocols involved all

he knew was that Parkinson had said no police, no heroes, no

drama. This was a long way from all of that.

From what Terry could tell them and from what they knew already

even the suits had to admit that it was a fantastic set up. A

'pipeline' that brought drugs into Europe all day every day in a

continual flow disguised in high class automobiles. And this was

only one market. Parkinson must be richer than Croesus.

Parkinson wasn't richer than Croesus, but he was getting there.

Whilst the European link had been the most lucrative by way of the

fact that Cherokees were going down real well in Europe, it was

only the beginning. In the months since the 'pipeline' had come on

stream Europe had been joined by Africa, South America and

Australasia would come on stream by Christmas. The ultimate irony

for Parkinson was for every Cherokee ordered by the UN half a kilo

of heroin flowed in to Africa. It was a sweat deal. It was just a

shame that they bought so much from the Japanese. If he'd set up

the 'pipeline' in the Shogun factory then we'd have seen some real

volume. Sure, he could have done without this whole Mason mess

but that was well on the way to being sorted. Mason and Harry

were held, the girl had to bring the briefcase now and the pipeline

had still been flowing uninterrupted for seven months.

It was a good point. Under normal circumstances (as if anything in

his line of work could be called normal) Parrish would take-over, play along with the kidnappers and then blow them all the way to kingdom come without harming any of the hostages. In the manual it was that easy but Parrish had never met a situation yet that ever looked remotely like the manual. This was no different. Too many hostages, to many players and one botched rescue attempt already. Parrish knew Parkinson held all the cards. The location for the handover had already been set and it was wholly against anywhere he would have chosen. Parrish , like Mason, liked open spaces. Great big open spaces. You could see people coming long they could see you and you could take them out any time you wanted. Parkinson's choice was anything but empty space. It was like they had been invited for tea. The address was a residential block in downtown Baltimore. From what he knew of the area it was on the way up with Europeans moving in and real estate prices rising. The houses ranged from modest two and three bedrooms to the larger three storey townhouses and the just plain opulent six bedrooms or more that he could never hope to afford. Parkinson's house was one of the three storey jobs and he had had it under surveillance for the last two hours.

Parrish had to admire Parkinson's choice. Too many people to be moved out, not enough to cover his men. Everybody would know everybody else and no matter how good your cover if you weren't meant to be there it would stick out like a sore thumb. A neighbourhood could only hide just so many hot dog guys and this place couldn't take any. Within that two hours Parrish knew that his men would already be in the neighbouring houses and across the street. But these were detached so there was no chance for spike mikes or cameras , they could get close but they couldn't see. Parkinson probably already knew they were there. Parrish prayed that he didn't, but with this many hostages Parkinson could afford to lose a few.

The Pipeline (11)

It was now or never, the radio crackled into life and with brief nods

all round fire broke out around the house. Explosions took out the

windows in front of them and anonymous men known only by

numbers swung off the roof and into the house. Smoke billowed

from the tears in the house whilst strong lights sought out the

friends and foes. Terry and Fay were knocked to the ground by the

first elements as the second and third wave entered the front and

back simultaneously. Small arms fire bristled briefly with single

pistol shots being met by short staccato busts of automatic fire and

the frenzied shouts of those inside. Terry struggled to free herself

from the burden above her screaming for Sean and yet feeling

every breath of the man above her, of whom she knew so little. She

could smell his very sweat and feel his every move .The coarse

fabric of his jacket had raked her face and even now she felt small rivulets of blood rising from the wound. She had never been so

close to a stranger . She seemed to have an eternity to consider the

ground beneath her and the man above her. His smell, his clothes,

his strength and yet all these thoughts passed by in an instant. Her

ribs ached and beside her Fay was struggling to overpower a similar

man as she screamed for her children and tore free from his grasp.

Instantly she was knocked down from behind and a second figure in

black covered her head and body beneath him as secondary bursts

of automatic fire ripped from the house and struck up a noisy

tattoo on the tarmac around them. The fire was returned from

behind them but this time it was single shots of a high calibre rifle

which screamed above their heads and tore into the flesh of the

man that had momentarily appeared at the second floor window.

As the bullet struck more automatic fire erupted from within the

house and the man was picked up by some unseen force and

dashed to the ground below.

Sean had always known it would come, he had just no way of knowing when. The muffled 'whump' of explosives was suddenly all around them and the temperature in the den seemed to rise by several degrees. Harry looked at him and they both knew they had less than two minutes to either live or die. Harry moved to cover the door whilst Sean stood to face anyone who would enter. He just hoped he looked like one of the good guys. In truth Sean knew that so long as you weren't 'carrying' you could probably survive but if you picked up a gun you were taken out, pure and simple. The door burst open and Sean faced one of the guards. His gun was brought up and aimed directly at him. There would be no happy ending. Harry kicked out at the door as the machine-pistol bucked in the guards' hands sending a stream of bullets across and up the wall shredding plaster and paper. As the guard readjusted the room exploded as two masked figures burst through the wall and shot simultaneously at the still incredulous guard who died in an instant . Searchlights split the room as Sean and Harry fell to the ground whilst their saviours moved on rapidly through and past them.

Sean gathered himself together and followed up the stairs past two

more bodies neatly shot through the head and into what had been

the living area. It now looked like a very bad day at the office but

Sean didn't recognise anybody who was down.

As suddenly as it had started, quiet descended on the suburban

street that moments before had resembled Beirut on a bad day.

Figures began to emerge from the house in ghostly silhouette

followed momentarily by the stark contrast of children in holiday

shirts running across the lawns towards them. Fay was up now,

tearing off the attention of her protector in black and charging

across the road to meet them tears streaming down her face and

collapsing under the onslaught of twin under-nines. Terry rose

uncertainly and began to walk towards the house unsure of what

she would find. Slowly at first and then with increasing speed and purpose she strode across the road, passing the daily reunion which today had added feeling and poignancy barely noticing the increasing numbers of shadowy figures coming towards her. She could hear screaming. Someone was screaming Sean's name at the top of their voice. Running hard for the door , she met Harry with blood trickling from a wound in his shoulder. Jean was cradling his arm but she couldn't tell if her tears were for Harry, Sean or herself. Terry crossed the threshold of the house which still stank of cordite and even now (surely it was hours since the bullets?) was still belching smoke and yet was still strangely silent save for the incessant screaming of some infernal woman.

Behind her , Peter had reached his wife and children and was cradling them - all desperate to touch and reassure, feel and be reassured. He was there in front of her, she grabbed him around the neck and she drew him to her. They fell towards the ground their tears mingling amidst a desperate search for each other and the recognition of an over powering need. Somewhere the woman

had stopped screaming.

Epilogue:

Andy turned in crisply, the V8 pulling strongly. God , he loved this part of the job and it was made all the better when the car he was driving was destined to be his own . In truth he hardly needed it but the promotion brought a 'job car' so who was he to turn down the Cherokee. Bronze metallic green the marketing boys called it but to him it was two tonnes, four doors, five litres, eight cylinders, forty grand's worth of four wheel drive power.

He turned back into the compound and drew up next up to Stan.

"Can I pick it up tomorrow"

"Sure thing"

Stan was a one-off . There was no one else like Stan in the entire plant, probably in the entire country. Stan had seen it all and whilst some had riled against changing work practices, longer shifts, 'associates', teamwork and all the other bullshit that seemed to be part of modern day manufacturing Stan had just taken it all in his stride knowing that when push came to shove all that really

mattered was the great god 'Volume'. So long as the metal went

out the gates nobody cared.

Stan took the keys and drove the Cherokee into the shop. He

flipped the bonnet, then dropped down out of the seat and walked

around to the back of the car. Under the rear cross member he

found what he was looking for and attached a small socket and

quickly lifted off the rear bumper. Checking around him quickly he

took out a small package and put it into his pocket.

Pension planning had never been like this at Ford.

Sean Mason,   Surname ½ way through

Harry
Steve Gaynor   first surname
Terry (she)

Louie Jameson
Barnes
Donnegan
Gaynor
Michaels

George Masters   Names first ltter
Nicky Inting   refered to surname
Stevie Barnes
Monkey

Little   1/3 in
Ao speaking between
characters ?

4339714